THE CHILDREN'S BOOK OF BOOKS 2000

In celebration of

WORLD BOOK DAY 2000

D0774377

Published in association with
MACMILLAN CHILDREN'S BOOKS

The organizers of World Book Day 2000 would like to thank the hundreds of publishers, booksellers, printers and authors all over the UK and the Republic of Ireland who have donated their time, money and, above all, enthusiasm for books and reading for pleasure to this important initiative. Particular thanks this year go to Book Tokens for their generous support of World Book Day 2000.

First published 2000 by Macmillan Children's Books
a division of Macmillan Publishers Limited
25 Eccleston Place, London SW1W 9NF
Basingstoke and Oxford
www.macmillan.co.uk

Associated companies throughout the world

ISBN 0 330 48243 2

The Children's Book of Books has been compiled and designed by Transworld Publishers with the help of Pam Royds of Scholastic Children's Books.

The generous support and assistance of the
following suppliers is particularly acknowledged:
Falcon Oast Graphic Art and Spot On Repro (typesetting and cover origination)
Clays Ltd (printing and binding) Stora Enso and Norske Skog (paper)

Welcome to the Children's Book of Books 2000!

This is the third year that World Book Day has been celebrated with a special book that you can buy with a free £1 Book Token.

This year the book is rather different. Here are nine stories and poems from nine brilliant writers which I guess you will read and want to keep and read again. Even so, they are just a small sample of the thousands of books that we shall all be reading on World Book Day and the days to come.

It's good to read!

Quentin Blake
Children's Laureate

ACKNOWLEDGEMENTS

William's Birthday by Richmal Crompton, adapted by Martin Jarvis from *Meet Just William*, original text copyright © Richmal C. Ashbee, adaptation copyright © Martin Jarvis 1986-98, illustrations copyright © Tony Ross 1999, published by Macmillan Children's Books.

Little Red Riding Hood and the Wolf by Roald Dahl from *Revolting Rhymes* copyright © Roald Dahl Nominee Ltd 1982, published by Jonathan Cape and Puffin Books.

Aliens Don't Eat Bacon Sandwiches by Helen Dunmore copyright © Helen Dunmore 1994, first published in *Fantastic Space Stories* (ed. Tony Bradman) by Doubleday and Corgi Books.

The Gift Pig by Joan Aiken from *A Harp of Fishbones and Other Stories* copyright © Joan Aiken 1972, illustrations copyright © Peter Bailey 1997, published by Jonathan Cape and Hodder Children's Books.

Into the Dark by Henrietta Branford, copyright © Henrietta Branford 1999, illustrations copyright © Mark Robertson 1999. From *Centuries of Stories* (ed. Wendy Cooling) published by Collins Children's Books.

Bridgey by Brian Jacques from *Seven Strange and Ghostly Tales* copyright © Brian Jacques 1991, published by Hutchinson Children's Books and Red Fox.

My Brother Gets Letters... by Michael Rosen from *Wouldn't You Like to Know* copyright Michael Rosen © 1977,1981 illustrations copyright © Quentin Blake 1977, 1982 published by Scholastic Children's Books.

The Gulf by Geraldine McCaughrean copyright © Geraldine McCaughrean 1999, first published in *Dare to be Different* by Bloomsbury Children's Books.

The Boy Who Walked on Water from *The Boy Who Walked on Water and Other Stories* text copyright © 1999 Vivian French. Illustrations copyright © 1999 Chris Fisher. Reproduced by permission of the publisher Walker Books.

CONTENTS

WILLIAM'S BIRTHDAY

Richmal Crompton
Adapted by Martin Jarvis
★ illustrated by Tony Ross ★

It was William's birthday, but, in spite of that, his spirit was gloomy and overcast. He hadn't got Jumble, his beloved mongrel, and a birthday without Jumble was, in William's eyes, a hollow mockery of a birthday.

Jumble had hurt his foot in a rabbit trap, and had been treated for it at home, till William's well-meaning but mistaken ministrations had caused the vet to advise Jumble's removal to his own establishment.

William had indignantly protested, but his family was adamant. And when the question of his birthday celebration was broached, feeling was still high on both sides.

'I'd like a dog for my birthday present,' said William.

'You've got a dog,' said his mother.

'I shan't have when you an' that man have killed it between you,' said William. 'He puts on their bandages so tight that their calculations stop flowin' an' that's jus' the same as stranglin' 'em.'

'Nonsense, William!'

7

'Anyway, I want a dog for my birthday present. I'm sick of not havin' a dog. I want another dog. I want two more dogs.'

'Nonsense! Of course you can't have another dog.'

'I said two more dogs.'

'You can't have two more dogs.'

'Well, anyway, I needn't go to the dancing-class on my birthday.'

The dancing-class was at present the bane of William's life. It took place on Wednesday afternoons – William's half-holiday – and it was an ever-present and burning grievance to him.

He was looking forward to his birthday chiefly because he took for granted that he would be given a holiday from the dancing-class. But it turned out that there, too, Fate was against him.

Of course he must go to the dancing-class, said Mrs Brown. It was only an hour, and it was a most expensive course, and she'd promised that he shouldn't miss a single lesson because Mrs Beauchamp said that he was very slow and clumsy and she really hadn't wanted to take him.

To William it seemed the worst that could possibly happen to him. But it wasn't. When he heard that Ethel's admirer, Mr Dewar, was coming to tea on his birthday, his indignation rose to boiling point.

'But it's my birthday. I don't want *him* here on my birthday.'

William had a deeply rooted objection to Mr Dewar. Mr Dewar had an off-hand, facetious manner which William had disliked from his first meeting with him.

* * *

William awoke on the morning of his birthday, still in a mood of unmelting resentment.

He went downstairs morosely to receive his presents.

His mother's present to him was a dozen new handkerchiefs with his initials upon each, his father's a new leather pencil-case. William thanked them with a manner of cynical aloofness of which he was rather proud.

'Now, William,' said his mother anxiously, 'you'll go to the dancing-class nicely this afternoon, won't you?'

'I'll go the way I gen'rally go to things. I've only got one way of goin' anywhere. I don't know whether it's nice or not.'

This brilliant repartee cheered him considerably. But still: no Jumble; a dancing class; *that* man to tea. Gloom closed over him again. Mrs Brown was still looking at him anxiously. She had an uneasy suspicion that he meant to play truant from the dancing-class.

When she saw him in his hat and coat after lunch she said again, 'William, you *are* going to the dancing-class, aren't you?'

William walked past her with a short laugh that was

wild and reckless and daredevil and bitter and sardonic. It was, in short, a very good laugh, and he was proud of it.

Then he swaggered down the drive, and very ostentatiously turned off in the opposite direction to the direction of his dancing-class. He walked on slowly for some time and then turned and retraced his steps with furtive swiftness.

To do so he had to pass the gate of his home, but he meant to do this in the ditch so that his mother, who might be still anxiously watching the road for the reassuring sight of his return, should be denied the satisfaction of it.

He could not resist, however, peeping cautiously out of the ditch when he reached the gate, to see if she were watching for him. There was no sign of her, but there was something else that made William rise to his feet, his eyes and mouth wide open with amazement.

There, tied to a tree in the drive near the front door, were two young collies, little more than pups. Two dogs. He'd asked his family for two dogs and here they were. Two dogs. He could hardly believe his eyes.

His heart swelled with gratitude and affection for his family. How he'd misjudged them! Thinking they didn't care two pins about his birthday, and here they'd got him the two dogs he'd asked for as a surprise, without saying anything to him about it. Just put them there for him to find.

His heart still swelling with love and gratitude, he went up the drive. The church clock struck the hour. He'd only just be in time for the dancing-class now, even if he ran all the way.

His mother had wanted him to be in time for the dancing-class and the sight of the two dogs had touched his heart so deeply that he wanted to do something in return, to please his mother.

He'd hurry off to the dancing-class at once, and wait till he came back to thank them for the dogs.

He stooped down, undid the two leads from the tree, and ran off again down the drive. The two dogs leapt joyfully beside him.

The smaller collie began to direct his energies to burrowing in the ditches, and the larger one to squeezing through the hedge, where he found himself, to his surprise, in a field of sheep.

He did not know that they were sheep. It was his first day in the country. He had only that morning left a London shop. But dim instincts began to stir in him.

William, watching with mingled consternation and delight, saw him round up the sheep in the field and begin to drive them pell-mell through the hedge into the road; then, hurrying, snapping, barking, drive the whole jostling perturbed flock of them down the road towards William's house.

11

William stood and watched the proceedings. The delight it afforded him was tempered with apprehension.

The collie had now made his way into a third field, in search of recruits, while his main army waited for him meekly in the road. William hastily decided to dissociate himself from the proceedings entirely. Better to let one of his dogs go than risk losing both . . .

He hurried on to the dancing-class. Near the front door he tied the collie to a tree with the lead, and entered a room where a lot of little boys – most of whom William disliked intensely – were brushing their hair and changing their shoes.

At last a tinkly little bell rang, and they made their way to the large room where the dancing-class was held. From an opposite door was issuing a bevy of little girls, dressed in fairy-like frills, with white socks and dancing-shoes.

There followed an attendant army of mothers and nurses who had been divesting them of stockings and shoes and outdoor garments.

William greeted these fairy-like beings with his most hideous grimace. The one he disliked most of all (a haughty beauty with auburn curls) was given him as a partner.

'*Need* I have William?' she pleaded. 'He's so *awful*.'

'I'm not,' said William. 'I'm no more awful than her.'

'Have him for a few minutes, dear,' said Mrs Beauchamp, who was tall and majestic and almost incredibly sinuous, 'and then I'll let you have someone else.'

The dancing-class proceeded on its normal course.

William glanced at the clock and sighed. Only five minutes gone. A whole hour of it – and on his birthday. His *birthday*. Even the thought of his two new dogs did not quite wipe out *that* grievance.

'Please may I stop having William now? He's doing the steps all wrong.'

William defended himself with spirit.

'I'm doin' 'em right. It's her what's doin' 'em wrong.'

Mrs Beauchamp stopped them and gave William another partner – a little girl with untidy hair and a roguish smile. She was a partner more to William's liking, and the dance developed into a competition as to who could tread more often on the other's feet.

It was, of course, a pastime unworthy of a famous Indian Chief, but it was better than dancing. He confided in her.

'It's my birthday today, and I've had two dogs given me.'

'*Oo!* Lucky!'

'An' I've got one already, so that makes three. Three dogs I've got.'

'Oo, I say! Have you got 'em here?'

'I only brought one. It's in the garden tied to a tree near the door.'

'Oo, I'm goin' to look at it when we get round to the window!'

They edged to the window, and the little girl glanced out with interest, and stood, suddenly paralysed with horror, her mouth and eyes wide open. But almost immediately her vocal powers returned to her.

'*Look!*' she said. 'Oh, *look*!'

They all crowded to the window.

The collie had escaped from his lead and found his way into the little girls' dressing-room.

There he had collected the stockings, shoes, and navy-blue knickers that lay about and brought them all out on to the lawn, where he was happily engaged in worrying them.

Remnants lay everywhere about him. He was tossing up into the air one leg of a pair of navy-blue knickers. Around him the air was thick with wool and fluff. Bits of unravelled stockings, with here and there a dismembered hat, lay about on the lawn in glorious confusion.

He was having the time of his life.

After a moment's frozen horror the whole dancing-class – little girls, little boys, nurses, mothers, and dancing-mistress – surged out on to the lawn.

The collie saw them coming and leapt up playfully, half a pair of knickers hanging out of one corner of his mouth, and a stocking out of the other.

They bore down upon him in a crowd. He wagged his tail in delight. All these people coming to play with him!

He entered into the spirit of the game at once and leapt off to the shrubbery, followed by all these jolly people. A glorious game! The best fun he'd had for weeks . . .

Meanwhile William was making his way quietly homeward. They'd say it was all his fault, of course, but he'd learnt by experience that it was best to get as far as possible away from the scene of a crime . . .

He turned the bend in the road that brought his own house in sight, and there he stood as if turned

14

suddenly to stone. He'd forgotten the other dog.

The front garden was a sea of sheep. They covered drive, grass and flower-beds. They even stood on the steps that led to the front door. The overflow filled the road outside.

Behind them was the other collie pup, running to and fro, crowding them up still more closely, pursuing truants and bringing them back to the fold.

Having collected the sheep, his instinct had told him to bring them to his master. His master was, of course, the man who had brought him from the shop, not the boy who had taken him for a walk. His master was in this house. He had brought the sheep to his master . . .

His master was, in fact, with Ethel in the drawing-room. Mrs Brown was out and was not expected back till tea-time.

Mr Dewar had not yet told Ethel about the two collies he had brought for her. She'd said last week that she 'adored' collies, and he'd decided to bring her a couple of them. He meant to introduce the subject quite carelessly, at the right moment.

And so, when she told him that he seemed to understand her better than any other man she'd ever met (she said this to all her admirers in turn), he said to her quite casually, 'Oh! By the way, I forgot to mention it but I just bought a little present – or rather presents – for you this afternoon. They're in the drive.'

Ethel's face lit up with pleasure and interest.

'Oh, how perfectly sweet of you,' she said.

'Have a look at them, and see if you like them.'

She walked over to the window. He remained in his armchair, watching the back of her Botticelli neck, lounging at his ease – the gracious, all-providing male. She looked out. Sheep – hundreds and thousands of sheep – filled the drive, the lawn, the steps, the road outside.

'Well,' said Mr Dewar, 'do you like them?'

She raised a hand to her head.

'What are they for?' she said faintly.

'Pets,' said Mr Dewar.

'*Pets!*' she screamed. 'I've nowhere to keep them. I've nothing to feed them on.'

'Oh, they only want a few dog biscuits.'

'*Dog* biscuits?'

Ethel stared at them wildly for another second, then collapsed on to the nearest chair in hysterics.

* * *

Mrs Brown had returned home. Mrs Brown had had literally to fight her way to the front door through a tightly packed mass of sheep.

Mr Dewar was wildly apologetic. He couldn't think what had happened. He couldn't think where the sheep had come from.

The other dog arrived at the same moment as a crowd of indignant farmers demanding their sheep. It still had a knicker hanging out of one corner of its mouth and a stocking out of the other.

William was nowhere to be seen.

William came home about half an hour later. There were no signs of Mr Dewar, or the dogs, or the sheep. Ethel and Mrs Brown were in the drawing-room.

'I shall never speak to him again,' Ethel was saying. 'I don't care whether it was his fault or not. I've told him never to come to the house again.'

'I don't think he'd dare to when your father's seen the state the grass is in. It looks like a ploughed field.'

'As if I'd want hundreds of *sheep* like that,' said Ethel, still confusing what Mr Dewar had meant to do with what he had actually done. '*Pets* indeed!'

'And Mrs Beauchamp's just rung up about the other dog,' went on Mrs Brown. 'It evidently followed William to the dancing-class and tore up some stockings and things there. I don't see how she can blame us for that. She really was very rude about it. I don't think I shall let William go to any more of her dancing-classes.'

William sat listening with an expressionless face, but his heart was singing within him. No more dancing-classes . . . that man never coming to the house any more. A glorious birthday – except for one thing, of course.

But just then the housemaid came into the room.

'Please, 'm, it's the man from the vet with Master William's dog. He says he's quite all right now.'

William leapt from the room, and he and Jumble fell upon each other ecstatically in the hall. The minute he saw Jumble, William knew that he could never have endured to have any other dog.

'I'll take him for a little walk. I bet he wants one.'

The joy of walking along the road again, with his beloved Jumble at his heels. William's heart was full of creamy content.

He'd got Jumble back. That man was never coming to the house any more.

He wasn't going to any more dancing-classes.

It was the nicest birthday he'd ever had in his life.

LITTLE RED RIDING HOOD
AND THE WOLF

Roald Dahl

As soon as Wolf began to feel
That he would like a decent meal,
He went and knocked on Grandma's door.
When Grandma opened it, she saw
The sharp white teeth, the horrid grin,
And Wolfie said, 'May I come in?'
Poor Grandmamma was terrified,
'He's going to eat me up!' she cried.
And she was absolutely right.
He ate her up in one big bite.
But Grandmamma was small and tough,
And Wolfie wailed, 'That's not enough!
'I haven't yet begun to feel
'That I have had a decent meal!'
He ran around the kitchen yelping,
'I've *got* to have another helping!'
Then added with a frightful leer,
'I'm therefore going to wait right here
'Till Little Miss Red Riding Hood
'Comes home from walking in the wood.'
He quickly put on Grandma's clothes,
(Of course he hadn't eaten those.)
He dressed himself in coat and hat.
He put on shoes and after that
He even brushed and curled his hair,

Then sat himself in Grandma's chair.
In came the little girl in red.
She stopped. She stared. And then she said,

'What great big ears you have, Grandma.'
'All the better to hear you with,' the Wolf replied.
'What great big eyes you have, Grandma,'
    said Little Red Riding Hood.
'All the better to see you with,' the Wolf replied.

He sat there watching her and smiled.
He thought, I'm going to eat this child.
Compared with her old Grandmamma
She's going to taste like caviare.

Then Little Red Riding Hood said, *'But Grandma,*
what a lovely great big furry coat you have on.'

'That's wrong!' cried Wolf. 'Have you forgot
'To tell me what BIG TEETH I've got?
'Ah well, no matter what you say,
'I'm going to eat you anyway.'
The small girl smiles. One eyelid flickers.
She whips a pistol from her knickers.
She aims it at the creature's head
And *bang bang bang*, she shoots him dead.
A few weeks later, in the wood,
I came across Miss Riding Hood.
But what a change! No cloak of red,
No silly hood upon her head.
She said, 'Hello, and do please note
'My lovely furry WOLFSKIN COAT.'

ALIENS DON'T EAT BACON SANDWICHES

Helen Dunmore

My brother Dan has been making his own bacon sandwiches since he was ten years old. It's not that he likes cooking that much – it's just that no-one else knows how to make the perfect bacon sandwich. He'd get everything ready by the cooker first. Bacon, bread, tomatoes, ketchup, sharp knife. The bacon had to be fried fast, so it was crisp but not dried up. He'd lay it on one slice of soft white bread, smear it with ketchup, cover it with tomato slices, and then clap a matching white slice on top. Then he'd bite into it while the bacon was hot and the fat was soaking into the bread. Dad used to say that Dan would go to Mars and back if he thought there'd be a bacon sandwich at the end of it. Don't forget this. The bacon sandwich is important.

Then there was the portable telephone. We should never have bought it, Mum said. I mean, I like talking to my friends on the phone, but Dan was something else. He was never off it. When he came in from school he'd pick up the phone right away and call someone he'd only been talking to half an hour before. And they'd talk and talk and talk. Sometimes Mum would come in and stand there tapping her watch or mouthing 'phone bill!' at him, but it never seemed to make much difference. Dan was a phone addict. I was cleaning my bike in the garden one day, and Mum and her friend Susie were talking about telephones and big bills and teenage kids. Susie said, 'It's all right as long as you realize that teenagers aren't people at all really. They're aliens from outer space. That's why they spend all their time on the phone. They have to keep in contact with other aliens who come from the same planet.'

I didn't take much notice of what Susie said at the time, but it came back to me later. Mum leaned back in her deckchair and laughed. She'd been out on a location all day, taking photographs: Mum's a photographer. She was working on a feature about corn circles. I expect you've seen pictures of them. Perfect circles in wheat, much too perfect to have been made by wind or rain. There were more of them than ever that year, and nobody knew how they came. At first the newspapers said it was a hoax. Reporters and photographers used to sit up and keep watch all night by cornfields, to catch the hoaxers. But they never did. Somehow they'd get sleepy and doze off and then when they jerked awake the circle would be there, just as round as if it had been drawn with a compass. Mum could have stayed the night too. She was working with a journalist friend who'd brought a tent along. Mum talked to Dan and me about it, then she decided not to stay. It was just a feeling she had that it wasn't a good idea. Dan and I always listened to Mum when she got feelings about things. Even I could remember how she'd said to Dad, just before he went on that last trip, 'Do be careful, love. I've got a feeling about it . . . I wish you weren't going.'

Dad had worked for INTERSTEL airways, on the crash investigation team. He was an instrument specialist. This time he hadn't been investigating a crash, but several pilots had reported interference with their instruments over the Mojave Desert. They'd managed to correct the problems manually so far, but the airline was quietly panicking. Dad had been working on a computer model, trying to find some pattern in what was going on. I don't remember much about that time, but Dan told me later that Dad had been up most of the night the week before he left. He was really worried. All he said to Dan and Mum was that a pattern kept coming up, and he didn't like the look of it.

Mum's feeling was right. Dad's plane crashed not far from Coyote Lake. Something went wrong with the instruments, they said: there'd been massive distortions caused by what looked like a powerful electrical storm. At least, that's what it looked like on the computer trace. But no storm showed up for hundreds of miles on the weather charts.

I asked Mum if she thought the corn circles really were made by aliens, like people said. She frowned, then she said. 'I don't know, Tony. I don't believe that the circles are made by UFOs landing. That would be much too obvious. The feeling I have is that we're being teased. Or tricked. As if someone – or something – is trying to distract us from what they're really doing.'

'What do you mean?'

'It's hard to explain, but try to put yourself in their

place. If there really are aliens trying to get a foothold on our planet, I think they'd do it in a way we'd hardly even notice. There'd be changes, but not huge ones. After all there are millions of us on this planet, and only a few of them. They'd come in very gradually over the years. They wouldn't want to risk being noticed – not too soon.'

'We'd be bound to notice, though, wouldn't we?'

'Not necessarily. Think of burglars. Some break in through the front door with crowbars, but others come in pairs pretending to be insurance salesmen. It's not till long after they've gone that you realize one of them's nipped upstairs and taken all your valuables. If there *were* aliens they wouldn't want to seem different. They'd want to seem like us. Part of normal life.'

So Mum thought the corn circles were there to keep us busy. To stop us noticing what else was going on. I shivered.

Dan was fifteen and a half, and I was almost eleven. You wouldn't think we'd be friends as well as brothers, but we always had been. Dan told me things he'd never tell Mum. He knew I'd never grass on him. And if something made him sad he could tell me that too. He had a music centre for his fifteenth birthday, much better than the one downstairs in the sitting-room. He'd lie on his bed and I'd lie on the floor and we'd listen to his music and he'd tell me about what was going on with his friends; not all of it, but some. Enough. Dan had a Saturday job, so he always had money. And he'd talk to me about Genevieve. He knew I liked her. He'd had girlfriends before, but Genevieve was different.

That was another clue I didn't pick up straightaway. It was about five o'clock and Dan and I were home from school, but Mum wasn't back yet. The phone rang and I answered it. It was Genevieve. She asked how I was, the way she always did. She even remembered that I'd had to take my budgie to the vet, and asked if he was OK now. Then she said, 'Is Dan there, Tony?'

'Yes, I'll just get him.'

I turned round. Dan was lounging in the doorway, watching me.

'It's Genevieve,' I said, holding out the phone, but Dan didn't take it. He just kept on looking at me. It's hard to describe what happened next. I hadn't really been thinking about what was going on, because I was just doing something I'd done loads of times before, taking a call for Dan and passing it on to him. And since it was Genevieve I knew he'd be pleased. But he wasn't pleased this time. He didn't react at all. I felt as if I was searching Dan's face for someone who wasn't there, like you'd search an empty house for a light in the windows.

'It's *Genevieve*!' I hissed, thinking perhaps he hadn't heard, and wishing I'd pressed the silence button in case Genevieve had. But Dan just shook his head, very slightly, as if he was making fun of me. Or Genevieve. And I was left holding the phone.

'I'm sorry, Genevieve,' I gabbled. 'He just went out, I think. I mean, I thought he was here, but he isn't.' It must have sounded like a lie, but Genevieve isn't a suspicious sort of person.

'Oh, that's OK, Tony,' she said. 'I'll try again later.

See you,' and she put the phone down. Her voice was just the same as always. You know how some people's voices make you feel that good things are about to happen? Genevieve had that sort of voice.

Dan's voice was cold and irritated. I couldn't believe I was hearing him right. 'I wish she'd stop bothering me,' he said.

'What?'

'You heard. I said I wish she'd stop bothering me. That girl really bugs me. If she calls again, say you don't know when I'll be back. No. Never mind. I'll take the phone.'

He held his hand out for it. Darkness looked out of his eyes, and blankness. There was no Dan there at all. He took the phone and held it up as if he was going to dial straightaway. The silver antenna poked out at the side of his head. I felt a shiver go through me. The antenna. Dan's dead eyes. Something scratched at the back of my mind, wanting to be let in:

'That's why they spend all their time on the phone, so they can keep in touch with all the other aliens . . .'

I stared at Dan and he stared back at me. Mocking, as if he knew something I didn't. And in a way . . . almost frightening. And then I heard Mum's key go into the front door lock.

Dan stopped looking at me. By the time Mum called hello to us, he was already on his way up the stairs, calling back 'Homework' as he went. That was strange, too. Dan usually made Mum a cup of coffee when she got in from work. His bedroom door banged with the sort of bang that tells everyone else to keep out. I waited to hear the music; Dan always turned on his music as soon as he got into his room. But nothing happened. It was absolutely silent, as if there was no Dan in there at all.

That was the first evening Dan didn't eat supper. He'd been into Burger King with Alex on his way back from school. Mum didn't bother about it: she was tired and upset because she and her journalist friend had had an argument with their editor. The editor didn't like the idea of aliens coming in secretly while we were all busy with the corn circles. He wasn't going to run the feature unless they changed it.

The next day Dan said he had to finish a piece of coursework and could he take a sandwich and a glass of milk up to his room. I don't remember all the excuses for not eating after that, at breakfast and tea and supper. They were never the same twice. Dan had always been clever, but now he was cunning too. He emptied his wastepaper basket every day now, so there was no chance of Mum finding the sandwiches he hadn't eaten. It was hard to know how much Mum had noticed. She never said anything, and she carried on giving Dan dinner money as usual.

It was three nights after the phone call from Genevieve that I couldn't sleep. My bedroom was next to Dan's, but I hadn't been into Dan's room for three days. Have you ever seen two magnets fighting one another with an invisible forcefield between them? There was one of those forcefields at Dan's bedroom door. You couldn't see it, you couldn't touch it, but it was there. Even Mum found excuses not to go in there. She was collecting the dirty washing one afternoon when Dan was late home, and she said, 'I ought to have a sock-search under Dan's bed,' but she didn't go in. She hesitated by his door, then she said, 'No. He's old enough to sort out his own dirty washing,' and she walked past into my room to change my duvet cover.

I kept turning over and over in bed. I was used to falling asleep to the sound of Dan's music, and I couldn't settle down in the silence. What was he doing? Was he sitting there? Reading? Working? I knew there wasn't anyone else in his room, though usually Dan had his friends round a lot, and often they stayed late. None of his friends had been round for the past three days. And I don't know what he'd said to Genevieve, but she hadn't called again. I tossed back the duvet and it flumped on to the floor. I found myself tiptoeing across the carpet, easing the door-handle down, pulling the door open very gently. The landing light was on. Everything was quiet and Mum's door was shut too. 12:37 on my watch. She'd be asleep. My heart thudded as I crept close to Dan's door. Yes, it was still there, the invisible hand pushing me away, saying I wasn't wanted there. But I wasn't going to take any notice this time. This was Dan, my brother. I took a breath, and touched his door-handle. Something fizzed on my fingers, like a tiny electric charge, like a rush of static electricity. I pulled my hand away and stepped back. Then I stopped myself.

'It's only Dan,' I told myself fiercely. 'It's only Dan.'

This time the prickle of electricity wasn't so bad, or perhaps it was because I was expecting it. Very gently I pushed the handle down. It didn't squeak or click. Then I pushed the door. As it opened a narrow strip of light fell from the landing into the darkness of Dan's room. It lit up Dan's bed, which was opposite the door. It lit up Dan, who was sitting up on the bed, fully dressed, reading. Reading in the dark. It lit up Dan's eyes as he turned to me, not at all surprised, as if he'd been expecting me. As if he'd seen me through the door.

'Hi,' he said, and turned a page.

There was only one switch for the main light, and it was by the door. It was off. I opened the door wider, so that more light came in, and walked across to Dan's bed. Casually, I touched his bedside light. It was cold. It hadn't been on at all. He'd really been reading in the dark – unless he'd been pretending? Unless he was trying to trick me and he'd been sitting there with the book, waiting for me to come in? But then how had he known I was going to come in?

There wasn't an answer. There was only Dan sitting on his bed. He didn't look as if he liked me much.

'I can't sleep,' I said. 'I'm going down to make some hot chocolate. Do you want some?'

'No,' said Dan. A week ago he'd have come down with me so I wouldn't make too much noise and wake up Mum. He'd have whipped up the chocolate, the way he does. Suddenly I had an idea.

'I'm going to make a bacon sandwich,' I said, and waited for Dan to say what he always said: 'You make a bacon sandwich? Don't make me laugh. Let the man from the army do it.' And then he'd make it for me.

He didn't. But something went over his face. Just for a second, there was a flicker of the real Dan, and as soon as I saw it I knew for sure that whoever else had been there the past three days, it hadn't been Dan.

Then his face went back to the not-Dan face. The alien face. I felt the back of my neck prickle. Maybe it was the electricity, tingling around the room. Out of the corner of my eye I caught a movement. It was the minute hand of Dan's electric wall-clock, racing crazily round and round in a perfect circle. The thing inside my brother looked straight at me, daring me to say what I'd seen. The prickle ran up my arms and down. I'd run into a storm, just the way Dad had done, only here it wasn't as strong. There was only one of them here. I shook my head to clear the buzzing of my thoughts. Dan needed me.

'I really fancy a bacon sandwich,' I said again. 'We've got all the stuff. White bread, tomatoes, ketchup – and Mum bought some back bacon yesterday.'

Something struggled in his eyes again, like the ghost of my brother. It wasn't winning. Dan wanted so much to come back, but he couldn't. There was something else there, something alien, and it was too strong for Dan. It meant to stay, and it meant to keep Dan out of his own body. But at least now I felt I knew what I was fighting. What we were fighting. Dan hadn't eaten anything for three days. I knew he hadn't. He must be hungry. Whatever was in him now didn't need food, not our earth food. But Dan did. And Dan would do anything for a bacon sandwich. Perhaps, if I could take him by surprise somehow, and get him to eat – could that break whatever power this thing had over him? I didn't know, but it was worth trying.

'See you downstairs if you change your mind,' I said.

Our neighbours have a baby which cries in the night, so Mum goes to bed with cotton wool in her ears. Even so, I moved quietly as I lit the gas, got out the heavy frying-pan, found bacon and tomatoes in the fridge, rummaged in the cupboard for ketchup. I just hoped the smell of frying bacon wouldn't wake her. I put the frying-pan on, melted a bit of fat, and lowered the bacon on the slice. It fizzled. After a minute the first tantalising wisp of the smell of frying bacon began to wreathe round the kitchen. Soon it would be through the door, then up the stairs, then under Dan's door. I turned up the heat carefully. I didn't want it to burn. The bacon spluttered, making a friendly sound in the kitchen. I laid the bread ready, and the sliced tomatoes, and the ketchup bottle. A drop of hot fat sparked on to the back of my hand and I sucked it away. Dan. Dan. Dan.

'Dan'd go to Mars and back if he thought he'd get a bacon sandwich at the end of it,' Dad used to say. That was before Dad went.

The kitchen door opened. Dan walked slowly, as if he was pushing through something heavy. His face was pale, and it wasn't smooth and hard any more, the way it had been the past three days. It looked crumpled, as if he was trying to remember something.

'Your sandwich is nearly ready,' I said. I took the bacon off the heat, slid the slices out of the pan and laid them across the bread. I layered on the tomato and squeezed out just the right amount of ketchup. Then I cut the sandwich in half. Dan watched me all the time. I lifted my half, and took a bite. I saw him lick his lips, but he was shivering, as if he felt cold. And things were moving behind his eyes, as if they were fighting for space there.

'Dan,' I said. 'Your sandwich is getting cold.'

His hands had dropped to his sides. They looked heavy. He didn't have the strength even to lift his hands, because all his strength was going into that fight inside him, between the Dan who was my brother and the stranger who wanted to make his home inside my brother's body. And that stranger was hanging on, tooth and claw. It wasn't going to let go easily. I knew now for sure that it was nothing human that was looking at me out of Dan's eyes. It had come from far away, and all it cared about was its resting-place. It was here for a purpose. It didn't care for Dan, or me or any of us. All it cared about was what it needed. Dan would never eat or sleep again if it had its way.

'Dan,' I said again. It felt as if his name was all I had. I came up close to him with his half of the sandwich still in my hand. He backed off a step or two, but then he didn't go any farther. I knew it was the real Dan who wanted to stay.

Suddenly I remembered something from far back, when I was sick with tonsilitis, not long after Dad died. It was when I was about six, I think. I had to take medicine four times a day, and I hated it. I used to press my lips tight shut and Mum couldn't make me swallow it. Then Dan took the spoon. He didn't seem worried, like Mum, and he didn't have any doubt that I'd open my mouth. He just put the spoon near my lips, without trying to push it into my mouth, and he said, 'Come on, babes. Do it for me.' And I did, every time, four times a day till I was better. The words had been like magic to me then, when I was a little kid. Would they work now? Could they be the one thing that would bring Dan back and help him to fight off that powerful and lonely thing which had come to make its home in him?

I held the bacon sandwich up to Dan's mouth. His face was sweaty and he was breathing hard, as if he'd been running a long way.

'Come on, babes,' I whispered. 'Do it for me.'

I held my breath. I said it again, but silently. Then, like something in slow motion, Dan's mouth opened. I could see how hungry he was. How much he wanted to come home. I felt the electric prickle again, the one I'd felt when I first tried to open Dan's door. It was stronger now. It was trying to beat up a storm. It was fighting me, as well as Dan. But this time it wasn't going to win. Dan bit down. He bit into the white bread, the bacon which was still hot, the juicy tomato. I saw the marks of his teeth in the bread. He chewed, and he swallowed the bacon sandwich. Then I looked at him and it was like looking at a house where all the lights have come on at once after it's been empty for a long time. His hands weren't heavy any more. He grasped the sandwich, bit again, and in a minute he'd finished it.

'You going to make me another, Tony, or have I got to show you how the man from the army makes a bacon sandwich?' he asked, and he smiled.

I didn't even jump when Mum opened the kitchen door. I knew it was her, not the thing which had been here and which was gone now, away through lonely space and places I couldn't begin to imagine, looking for somewhere else to make its home. Mum pulled the cotton wool out of her ears.

'You boys,' she said. 'I should have known. I was dreaming about bacon sandwiches.'

* * *

I don't know how Dan made it up with Genevieve, but the next day she was round at our house again. Dan's bedroom door was open, and his music was throbbing through the house. Mum didn't tell him to turn it down. She was in a wonderful mood because the editor had rung her back. He'd changed his mind and he was going to run the story about the corn circles in the way Mum and her friend wanted. For some reason he'd suddenly come to think it was worth printing the theory about aliens operating like bogus insurance salesmen, distracting us with corn circles and stealing our valuables when we weren't looking.

I asked Mum, 'Does the editor have kids?'

'Yes, he's got a teenage daughter. She's been a bit of a problem lately, apparently – he was telling me.' Mum glanced round, saw Dan was laughing with Genevieve, and whispered, 'His daughter's been acting a bit like Dan has these past few days, I think. But he says she's got over it, too.'

Genevieve stayed to supper, and you can guess what we ate. While we were eating it, I thought of what had happened the night before, in our midnight kitchen.

'Aliens don't eat bacon sandwiches,' I thought, looking at my brother.

THE GIFT PIG

Joan Aiken

★ illustrated by Peter Bailey ★

Once there was a king whose queen, having just presented him with a baby princess, unfortunately died. The king was very upset at this, naturally. But he had to go on with the arrangements for the christening just the same, as court etiquette was strict on this point. What with his grief and distraction, however, and the yells of his daughter, an exceedingly lively and loud-voiced infant, the invitations to the christening were sent out in a very haphazard manner, and by mistake two elderly fairies were invited who were well known to loathe one another, so that when they met there was bound to be trouble, though when encountered separately they were pleasant enough.

The day of the christening arrived and at first all went well. The baby princess was christened Henrietta and behaved properly at the ceremony, crying a little but not too much. Then the whole party of relatives and guests strolled back from the royal chapel to the throne room where the reception was being held; the king noticed with alarm that the two elderly fairies were walking side by side. They seemed to be nodding in the most friendly way, but when he edged nearer to them he heard one say, 'How very well you are looking, darling Grizel! One wouldn't – by artificial light – take you for a day over two hundred.'

'Hardly surprising since I celebrated my hundred-and-eightieth birthday last week. But how are *you*, dear Bella? Do you think it was wise to attend the service in that draughty chapel? You walk with such a limp these days.'

'I am perfectly well, thank you, my love. And one does have one's social duty.'

'Especially when there is a free meal attached to it, tee hee!'

'But I confess I hardly expected to see you here – I understood the king's friends were all intelligent and – well, you know – *creative* people.'

'Creative, my angel? In that case, do tell me how *you* qualify for admission?'

Shuddering, the poor king made haste to cut the cake and circulate the sherry in hopes of sweetening these acid ladies. He wished that he could get rid of them before the visitors began to give their christening presents, but saw no way to.

Presently the guests, fairy and otherwise, having eaten every crumb of cake and drunk all the sherry, began depositing their gifts and taking their leave. The baby, pink and good in her cradle, was given whole rooms full of silver and coral rattles, shoals of shawls, bonnets and bootees by the bushel, mounds of matinee jackets and mittens, stacks of embroidered smocks and knitted socks. Besides this, she was endowed with good health, a friendly and cheerful nature, intelligence, and a logical mind.

Then the fairy Bella stepped forward and, smiling at the king, said, 'You must forgive me if my wish is not quite so pleasant as some of the preceding ones, but meeting – ahem – such very *odd* company in your palace has made me nervous and brought on a migraine. Let the princess rue the day that someone gives her a pig, for if ever that happens she will turn into a pig herself.'

'Moreover,' said the fairy Grizel, coming to the other side of the cradle, 'she will marry somebody with no heart and only one foot.'

'Excuse *me*, dear, I hadn't finished yet; if you could kindly give me time to speak. The princess will lose her inheritance—'

'I *beg* your pardon; I was going to say that there will be a revolution—'

'*Will* you please be quiet, madam! There will *not* be a revolution – or at least, the princess herself will be lost long before that occurs – she will be poor and unknown and have to work for her living—'

'She'll marry one who has spent all his life in the open—'

'Oh, for gracious' sake! Didn't I just say she would marry somebody with only one foot?'

'The two things are not incompatible.'

'You don't very often find agricultural workers with only one foot.'

'Ladies, ladies!' said the king miserably, but not daring to be too abrupt with them, 'you have done enough harm to my poor child! Will you please continue your discussion somewhere else?'

The feuding fairies took their leave (so exhausted by

their exhilarating quarrel that they both went home, retired to bed, and died next day) while, left alone, the poor king hung with tears in his eyes over his beautiful pink baby wondering what, if anything, could be done to avert the various bits of evil fortune that were coming to her. All that seemed to lie in his power was strict censorship of her presents, so as to make sure that she was never given a pig.

This he managed successfully until she was five years old, when her cousin came to stay with her. Lord Edwin Fitzlion was a spoilt, self-willed boy of about the same age as the princess; he was the seventh son of a seventh son; his brothers were all much older and had gone off into the world, his father had taken to big-game hunting and hardly ever came home, while his mother, tired of looking after boys and attending to shirts, schools, boots, and bats was away on a three-year cruise. Lord Edwin had been left in the care of servants.

He was very beautiful, with dark velvety eyes and black hair; much better looking than his fat pink cousin; he was inclined to tease her. One day he overheard two equerries discussing the prophecies about her, and he became consumed with curiosity to see whether she would really turn into a pig if she were given one.

There were considerable difficulties about bringing pigs into the palace, but finally Edwin managed to buy a small one from a heavily bribed farmer. He smuggled it in, wrapped in brown paper and labelled *Inflatable rubber dinghy with outboard pump attachment*. Finding the nursery empty he undid the pig and let it loose, then rushed in search of Henrietta.

'Henry! come quick, I've brought a present for you.'

'Oh, where?'

'In the nursery! Hurry up!'

With rare politeness he stood aside to let her go in first and heard her squeak for joy as she ran through the door, 'Oh, it's a dear little pig—'

Then there was silence, except for more squeaks, and when Lord Edwin looked through the door he saw two little pigs, absolutely identical, sniffing noses in the most friendly way.

Lord Edwin was sent home in disgrace to his father's castle, where he proceeded to run wild, as his parents were still away. (In fact they never returned.) He spent all his time in the woods, riding his eldest brother's horse, Bayard, and flying his next brother's falcon, Ger. One day when far from home he saw a large hare sitting upright on the other side of a pool. Quickly he unhooded the falcon and prepared to fly her.

The hare said, 'You'll be sorry if you do that.'

'Oh, who cares for you,' said Edwin rudely, and he loosed Ger. But the falcon, instead of towering up and dropping on the hare, flew slantwise across the pond into some thick trees and vanished from view. Edwin's eyes followed the bird in annoyance and perplexity. When he looked back he saw that a little old man with an unfriendly expression was standing on the spot where the hare had been.

'You are a spoilt, ill-mannered boy,' the old man said. 'I know all about you and what you did to your cousin. You can stay where you are, learning a bit of patience and consideration, until a Home Secretary comes to rescue you.'

Nobody had been particularly fond of Edwin, so nobody missed him or inquired after him.

The king, of course, was heartbroken when he learned what had happened to his daughter. Numerous tests were carried out on the two little pigs, in an attempt to discover which one was the princess. They were put in little beds with peas under the mattresses but both rummaged out the peas and ate them in the course of the night. Dishes of pearls and potato-peelings were placed in front of them, in the hope that the princess would prefer the pearls, but they both dived unhesitatingly for the potato-peelings. The most eminent pig-breeders of the kingdom were brought in to scrutinize them, but with no result; they were two handsome pink little pigs, and that was all that could be said of them.

'Well,' said the king at length, 'one of them is my daughter, and she must receive the education due to a princess. Some day I suppose she will be restored to her proper shape, as she is to marry a one-footed man, poor dear—'

'The fairy didn't actually say a *man* with one foot,' pointed out the Lord Chamberlain.

'Use your sense, man. What else could it be? Anyway she must have a proper education. It would never do if when she reverted to human shape she knew no more than a child of five.'

So the little pigs sat seriously side by side on two little chairs in the schoolroom and were taught and lectured at by a series of learned professors and eminent schoolmistresses. No-one could tell if any of this teaching sank in, for they merely sat and gazed. If asked questions, they grunted.

One day when the pigs were nearly fifteen, the king came into the schoolroom.

'Hullo, my dears,' he said, 'how are you this morning?' He patted his daughter and her friend, then sat down wearily in an armchair to rest while they had their lunch. Affairs of state were becoming very burdensome to him these days.

A footman brought in two big blue bowls of pig-mash, one in each hand. The pigs began to give piercing squeals and rush about frantically, bumping into tables and chairs and each other. Their attendant firmly collared them one at a time, tied a white napkin round the neck of each, and strapped them into two chairs. The bowls were put in front of

them and instantly there was such a guzzling and a slupping and a splashing and a slobbering that nobody could hear a word for five minutes until the bowls were empty. Then the little pigs looked up again, beaming with satisfaction, their faces covered in mash.

The footman solemnly stepped forward again and wiped their faces clean with a cloth-of-gold flannel. Then they were let out to play, and could be seen through the window whisking about the palace garden with tails tightly curled, and chasing one another across the flower-beds.

The king sighed.

'It's no use,' he said, 'one must face facts. My daughter Henrietta is *not* an ordinary princess. And her friend Hermione is a very ordinary little pig. I am afraid that no prince, even a one-footed one, would ask for Henrietta's hand in marriage after seeing her eat her lunch. We must send them to a finishing school. They have had plenty of intellectual education – at least I suppose they have – it's time they acquired a little polish.'

So the two pigs were packed off (in hampers) to Miss Dorothea ffoulkes' Select Finishing School for the Daughters of the Aristocracy and Nobility.

At first all went well. The king received monthly reports which informed him that his daughter (and her friend) had learned to walk downstairs with books on their heads, to enter and leave rooms, get in and out of motor cars with grace and dignity, play the piano and the harp, waltz, cha-cha-cha, embroider, and ride side-saddle.

'Well, I've always heard that Miss ffoulkes was a marvel,' said the king, shaking his head with astonishment, 'but I never thought anyone could teach a pig to ride side-saddle. I can't wait to see them.'

But he had to wait, for Miss ffoulkes strictly forbade the parents of her pupils to visit them while they were being put through her course of training. The reason for this was that she had to treat the girls with such frightful severity, in order to drill the necessary elegance and deportment into them, that if they had been given the chance they would have implored their parents to take them away. Letters, however, were always written to the dictation of Miss ffoulkes herself, so there was no opportunity of complaining, and at the end of her course the debutantes were so grateful for their beautiful poise that all was forgotten and forgiven.

Miss ffoulkes nearly met her Waterloo in Henrietta and Hermione though. She managed to teach them tennis, bridge, and how to dispose of a canapé stick, but she could not teach them flower-arrangement. The pigs had no taste for it; they always ate the flowers.

One day they had been spanked and sent into the garden in disgrace after it was discovered that they had eaten a large bundle of lilies and asparagus-fern which they were supposed to build into a decorative creation. Sore and miserable they wandered down Miss ffoulkes's dreary gravel paths. Simultaneously they were seized by the same impulse. They wriggled through the hedge at the bottom of the garden and were seen no more at the Select School.

Instead of a final report on deportment the king had a note from Miss ffoulkes which said, 'I regret to announce that your daughter and her friend have committed the unpardonable social blunder of running away from my establishment. The police have been informed and will no doubt recover them for you in due course. Since this behaviour shows that our tuition has been thrown away on them your fees are returned herewith. (Cheque for £20,000 enc.) Your very obdt. srvt. Dorothea ffoulkes.'

In spite of all efforts, the police failed to trace the two little pigs. Advertisements in newspapers, on television and radio, pictures outside police stations, offers of rewards, brought no replies. The king was in terror, imagining his daughter and her friend innocently strolling into a bacon factory. He gave up all pretence at governing and spent his time in a desperate round of all the farms in the kingdom, gazing mournfully at pig after pig in the hope of recognizing Henrietta and Hermione. But none of the pigs responded to his greetings.

As a matter of fact Henrietta and her friend had gone no farther than the garden of the house next door to Miss ffoulkes. There they had been rooting peacefully (but elegantly because their training had not been wasted) among the roses near the front gate when a young man in a white coat came out of the house, irritably listening to the parting words of a beautiful young lady with flowing dark hair.

'And don't forget,' she was saying earnestly, 'all your last experimental results are in the stack under the five-gramme weight, and the milk for tea is in the test-tube at the left-hand end of the right-hand rack, and the baby amoeba wants feeding again at five. Now

I really must fly, for my fiancé becomes very annoyed if he is kept waiting.'

'Goodbye, Miss Snooks,' said the white-coated young man crossly, and he slammed the gate behind her. 'Why in the name of goodness do all my assistants have to get married? Not one of them has stayed longer than three months in the last three years.'

Then his eye fell on two pigs, who were gazing at him attentively.

'Pigs,' he mused. 'I wonder if pigs could be taught to do the work? Pigs might not be so prone to become engaged. Pigs, would you consider a job as research assistants?'

The pigs liked his face; they followed him into the house, where he instructed them in the research work he was doing on cosmic rays.

'I shall have to teach you to talk, though,' he observed, 'for I can't put up with assistants who grunt all the time.'

He laid aside all his other work and devoted himself to teaching them; at the end of a week he had succeeded, for he was the most brilliant scientist and philosopher in the kingdom. In any case, nobody had ever considered teaching the pigs to talk before.

When they could speak the professor asked their names.

'One of us is Henrietta and one is Hermione, but we are not sure which is which,' they told him, 'for we were muddled up when we were young.'

'In that case I shall call you Miss X and Miss Y. Miss X, you will look after making the tea, feeding the amoeba, and filing the slides. Miss Y, you will turn away all visitors, keep the cosmic ray tuned, and polish the microscope. Both of you will make notes on my experiments.'

The two pigs now found their education of great value. They could carry piles of books and microscope slides about on their heads, curtsy gracefully to callers as they showed them the door, write notes in a neat little round hand, and play the piano and the harp to soothe the professor if his experiments were not going well. They were all very happy together, and the professor said that he had never before had such useful and talented assistants.

One day after about five years had passed in this manner, the professor raised his eye from the microscope, rubbed his forehead, looked at Miss Y, industriously taking notes, and Miss X, busily putting away slides, and said, 'Pigs, it occurs to me to wonder if you are really human beings turned into your present handy if humble form?'

'One of us is,' replied Miss Y, tucking her pencil behind her, 'but we don't know which.'

'It should be easy to change you back,' the professor remarked. 'I wonder I never thought of it before. We can just switch on the cosmic ray and rearrange your molecules.'

'Which of us?'

'You can both try, and I daresay nothing will happen to one of you.'

'Should we like that?' said the pigs to each other. 'You see we're used to being together,' they told the professor.

'Oh, come, come,' he exclaimed impatiently. 'If one of you is really human, it's her plain duty to change back, and the other one should not stand in her way.'

Thus admonished, both pigs walked in front of the ray, and both immediately turned into young ladies with pink faces, turned-up noses, fair hair, and intelligent blue eyes.

'Humph,' remarked the professor, 'that ray must be more powerful than I had allowed for; we do not seem to have advanced matters much farther.'

As the young ladies still did not know which of them was which, they continued to be called Miss X and Miss Y, and as they were very happy in their work they continued to help the professor.

One day Miss Y noticed a number of callers approaching the front door. Though she curtsied politely and did her best to turn them away, they insisted on entering the laboratory.

'Professor,' said a spokesman, 'we are the leaders of the Revolution, and we have come to invite you to be the first president of our new republic, since you are undoubtedly the wisest man in the country.'

'Oh good gracious,' said the professor, very much taken aback and frowning because he hated interruptions to his work, 'whatever possessed you to revolt, and what have you done with the king?'

'We revolted because it is the fashionable thing to do – all the other countries have done it ages ago – and the king retired last week; he has taken to farming. But now please step into the carriage which is waiting outside and we will escort you to the president's residence.'

'If I accept,' said the professor, 'it is understood that I must have unlimited time to pursue my research.'

'Yes, yes, you will need to do very little governing, just keep an eye on things and see that justice and reason prevail. Of course you can appoint anybody you choose to whatever government positions you wish.'

'In that case I shall appoint my two assistants, Miss X and Miss Y, to be the Home and Foreign Secretaries. I am certain that no-one could be more competent.'

The new president's residence turned out to be none other than the castle of the Baron Fitzlion, long since deserted. Here the republican government was set up, and as none of the old officials had been removed from their posts, everything proceeded very smoothly, and the professor and his two assistants found ample time to continue their research on cosmic rays.

They were now investigating the use of the professor's ray projector on plant life; one day Miss X took a small portable projector into the woods nearby, proposing to make notes about differences in the ray's effect on coniferous and deciduous trees.

While scribbling in her notebook she heard a sneeze, and looked up to discover that a larch in front of her had developed a head. Two handsome black eyes gazed at her mournfully.

'Are you the Home Secretary?' the head inquired.

'Why, yes,' replied Miss X, controlling her natural surprise at such a question being put to her by a tree.

'In that case would you be so extremely kind as to liberate the rest of me with your camera, or whatever it is?'

'I'm afraid this portable projector isn't strong

enough for that – it only runs off a battery. We shall have to build a larger one beside you and connect it to the mains; that will take two or three weeks.'

He sighed. 'Oh well, I've been here fifteen years, I daresay I can wait another three weeks. No doubt I deserved this fate for turning my poor little cousin into a pig, but I *am* so stiff.'

'Did you turn your cousin into a pig?' said Miss X with interest. 'I suppose that might have been me.'

'Were you turned into a pig?'

'Somebody was; we cannot be sure if it was my friend Miss Y or myself. You see, we are not certain which of us is which.'

'Henrietta was to lose her inheritance and go through a revolution.'

'So she has.'

'And be poor and unknown and earn her living.'

'We both are and do.'

'And marry a man with one foot. I'll tell you what,' said Lord Edwin, who had rapidly developed a tremendous admiration for Miss X's cheerful pink face and yellow hair – such a refreshing contrast to the leaves and branches which were all he had had to look at for the last fifteen years – 'I've only got one foot just now, you're standing on it; so if you marry me it will prove that you are the princess.'

'That's true,' she said thoughtfully, 'and then I shall be able to go and see poor Papa and tell him that I am me; there didn't seem much point in disturbing him until I had some more data.'

So the marriage ceremony between Lord Edwin and Miss X was performed while they were building the full-size cosmic ray projector nearby, and as soon as the bridegroom had been released they went to see the king, who was very contented on his farm and had no wish at all to resume governing.

'I have acquired a fondness for pigs after looking at so many,' he said. 'I am sure young people can manage very well without me.'

So Lord Edwin became Prime Minister (having learned thoughtfulness and civilized behaviour during his long spell in the woods). Miss Y, who was now known to be Hermione, married the professor, and they all governed happily ever after.

INTO THE DARK

Henrietta Branford
★ illustrated by Mark Robertson ★

I was born out of doors, I think, under the tall green bracken or out on the bee-singing heather. My mother loved such places. She died when I was very small but I remember her. She loved me and held me close. She did not want to leave me. She was one of the lake people, and our house was built on stilts, over the water. All night the lake lap-lapped under our floor.

When my mother died I was taken in by a woman called Marne who moved me away from the lake to live beyond the forest. I got no love from her – cold food and a cold heart, that was her way. Blows and curses. Goban, her man, was worse. Many's the time I thought he'd kill me. I used to think that if I did what they wanted, they would take to me, but they never did. They wanted my labour, not me.

50

That's why they sent me to carry the warning. It was a simple message: the Romans are coming, clanking up the hillsides, tall as giants. This is our land, but their general Hadrian has ordered the building of a great wall across it, to keep us away. It never will. They may be powerful and strong, with their gods and their roads and their long, long marches, but this is our land and we'll keep it.

I was to run to the lake. They said I must run all night and not stop until I'd warned the lake people. I said: 'It will be night time, and dark.' They laughed.

Marne and Goban were grabbing what they could carry and running north almost before I left them. 'How will I find you when I'm done?' I asked. They didn't answer.

'Head for the river and sundown,' the head man told me. 'Cross where the rocks make stepping-stones. Follow the stream through the wood. You'll find the village on an island in a lake.'

He did not give me a knife or a spear. I had no wool cloak and no shoes either. I do not like the dark. It presses on me and makes me afraid. The spirits of the dead love darkness. So do the priests, whom everybody fears. Also the wolf and the boar and the bear.

As I left the village, mad Mab tottered out of her hut and laid her bony hand on my head. She wiped a sign on to my forehead with her thumb. Writing is forbidden to us. Only the priests may write. I felt afraid, but I trusted her, because on those nights when Marne threw me out, or when I had to run from Goban's fist, I ran to Mab and she would let me in. Mostly she had no food and no fire, but she let me stay with her. I said

51

goodbye to her and she kissed me. Then I ran towards the river.

Smell of the bog myrtle as I push through the bushes. Smell of mint, and the water close by. I reach the river just as dusk wraps the land in mystery. The rocks are slippery and the water's deep. Water will suck you under if it can. Wait until the sun is gone. Now the sky is red like blood. Fish rise to catch the last of the dancing flies. Deer step out of the wood to drink at the river. Maybe an old grey wolf follows behind. Watch where the evening star will rise.

That star will show me the way. They told me not to stop but how can you run if you don't know the way? *Moonlight, starlight, bad'uns won't come out tonight.* I think my mother taught me that. Here is my star now. Look to the oak tree. Mark where the sun goes down. See where the star comes up. Now run.

Deer scatter when I stand. The dark is thicker now. River plants, cold under my foot, give off a good clean scent.

I run under the trees and the dark is all around me. These are yew trees. When the priests cut mistletoe from the yew they sacrifice to Lugh. I don't want their sacred knives digging in my entrails.

Water beside me. Look for the star in every clearing. Run until my lungs hurt and my heart hammers. Stop, breathing hard and loud. Quiet, quiet. I'll sit and rest a moment. I hear the song of water over the stones. My eyes close. Only for a moment. Then I'll run again.

Wake to the sound of footfalls in the dark. Two priests come down to the water. No-one can hide from them, they can see in the dark. What will they do to me? I make myself small and quiet and pray to Macha our mother to protect me. They lean over the water, killing something small they take from a sack. When they have finished they go back the way they came. They don't want me. I stand up, stretch, and run.

Wolves call to one another in the moonlight, long, shivering wails. I run under holly trees, the prickles sting my bare feet. After the prickle is out, the sting remains. I will run round them. Where is the water? I have lost the stream. The wolves are coming close, very close. Is it me they're hunting?

A yip in the dark, ahead of me. Another behind me. Climb like a cat up the ivy on a big oak tree. I sit on a broad branch, high above the pathway, with my legs drawn up tight. An old grey wolf trots out of the bracken. He stands under my tree, looking up. Moonlight shines on his long teeth. His mate comes out from under the bracken and stands beside him, staring at me. She is asking me a question but I don't know what it is. Now comes a long cry, a hunting cry, from off behind. Old man wolf and his mate run away into the darkness. It wasn't me they wanted.

I sit in the tree, shaking. From here I can see past the wood and down into the valley. There's a fire down there. Firelight shines on the helmets of the Romans. They clothe themselves in iron, it makes them hard to kill. I must move quietly. If they catch me they'll kill me. If they kill me, the lake people die too. I want to stay safe in my tree. I want to warn my mother's people. I want to hide. I want to run. Cloud covers the moon, the wood grows pitchy black. Down in the valley the fire glows red. Goban would stay in this tree.

Goban has no pride, no courage, no love for anyone. But I am not like him. I remember how my mother loved me.

I scrabble down the ivy. The moon sails out to light my way. I run down to the valley, moving quietly, carefully round the camp. A dog barks. Guards pace inside their palisade. They do not see the boy running past in the dark.

Ahead, the lake shines like a silver dish. I stand and stare while my fear and my anger and my sorrow rise in my chest and take my breath away. I think of my mother, take a deep breath and run downhill and out on to the wooden causeway. My feet thud, the wood is wet, I trip and roll over. I have not fallen all my long run, but now I fall like a fool, thumping down on my arse, ringing the wooden causeway like a bell.

A man runs out and hauls me up by the elbow. He brings his spear up under my chin. 'Who are you?' he whispers. 'Tell me, before I kill you.' His spear pricks sharp into my neck.

Before I can answer, a door opens in a house close by and a woman steps out. She walks over to where I crouch, the spear at my neck. She puts out her hand to trace the sign on my forehead. 'Leave him,' she says. 'He's a friend.'

'I'm from beyond the wood,' I say. I do not tell them that I came from here, once. 'I've run all night.'

'What for?' asks the woman. The man's spear is close to my neck still.

'To tell you the Romans are coming. They're camped close by the valley. I was sent to give you time to run.'

'Run now, fight later,' says the man. He takes his

spear away from my neck. 'What kind of people send a boy, alone and unarmed, without shoes on his feet, to warn their neighbours of danger?' he asks. The woman shakes her head and sighs. I feel ashamed.

After that the man put his hand on my shoulder and brought me indoors. His name was Vran. He gave me food and I sat in the warm, eating and drinking, while Vran spoke to the woman. When they went out to wake the village, I slept. I dreamed I had a proper home, where I could sit by the fire and eat when I was hungry. A stupid dream, I thought when I woke up.

Vran came in soon after. 'We're going now,' he said.

'So am I,' I answered.

He looked at me. 'I see a boy with nowhere good to go,' he said. 'I know that look.'

That was a long while back. I am at home in Vran's house now – one of the Lake people again. But I still remember running through the dark, and meeting Vran on the causeway.

BRIDGEY

Brian Jacques

'Sure and aren't ducks the greatest things in all the world!' Bridgey spoke her thoughts aloud to the white mists as they curled in wraithlike tendrils across the surface of the morning lake. The ducks ignored her completely, quacking and yammering the day's business among themselves as they waddled and trundled fussily into the water, led by Rafferty, the leader of the drakes.

Bridgey wiggled the toes of her bare feet in the mud at the water's edge as she talked to them. The ducks were used to the sound of the little girl's voice. 'Now don't stray too close by those bushes on the other side. Who knows, some divvil of a fox or ferret might devour you, feathers and all.'

Rafferty began paddling over to the very spot Bridgey had warned them about. She stamped her foot, causing mud to splatter the frayed hem of her skirt, and waving a willow twig at the drake, she called out, 'Mister Rafferty, are you deaf or just disobedient? What've I told you? Get out of there this very instant!'

Rafferty did a stately turn, cruising out into the centre of the lake, with an ill-assorted two score followers in his wake. Bridgey was still shaking the stick in reprimand.

'And stay away from there, d'ye hear me, or I'll tickle your tail with this stick, so I will. Wipe that silly smile off your beak, Mister Rafferty, and that goes for the rest of you. Stay this side, where I can see you well. The lake's safe, sure there's only the ould Grimblett down there – he watches over little maids and disobedient ducks good enough, 'tis his job.'

'Bridgey!'

She flinched momentarily at the sound of her uncle's voice.

'I'm over here by the lake, Uncle Sully.'

Sully McConville trod gingerly through the mud to his small niece.

'Have y'cleaned the duckpens out, girl?'

'I have so, while you were still abed.'

'Less of your lip. How many eggs today?'

'Seven and twenty, Uncle.'

Bridgey smelled the raw whiskey on her uncle's breath as he brought his unshaven face close to her. McConville's bleary red-veined eyes shifted slyly as he grabbed the willow twig from Bridgey's hand.

'Are y'telling me the truth now?'

'I am so, Uncle Sully.'

He twitched the stick close to her nose.

'If you're lyin' I'll skelp the skin off your bones, girl. I think you're going soft in the head, talking to yourself out here. What's all this about a Grimblett?'

Bridgey remained silent in the face of her uncle's sour temper. Sully growled at the mud which had seeped in through his leaky boot soles.

'Go on up to the house now. Put the kettle on for tea and boil me two eggs in it, no, make that three. I'll be taking the other two dozen in to sell at Ballymain market. Cut me three slices of white bread and put the honey jar on the table. Move yourself now!'

He snapped the twig and hurled it out into the lake, causing the ducks to quack and swim off in a half flutter. Digging a broken yellowed clay pipe out of his vest pocket Sully sucked on it. He spat noisily into the lake, calling after the girl, 'And you know what you'll get if I catch you eatin' eggs, honey or white bread, me lady.'

Bridgey called back cheerfully, 'Aye, so I do. You'll skelp the skin off me bones!'

She busied herself around the ill-equipped kitchen of the crumbling cottage, murmuring to herself happily. 'Oho, Sully McConville, don't you think yourself the big bold man now. But you'll find that you can't throw broken sticks or spit into the Grimblett's lake without the creature himself knowing it. Sure, wasn't I a witness to the whole thing meself, to say nothing of Mister Rafferty and his ducks. Small wonder they were all smilin' to themselves. Finer men than yourself haven't got away with less.'

The kettle was bubbling merrily as Bridgey spooned three duck eggs into the water. Facing the open window, she laid the well-scrubbed wooden table with white bread and a brownstone crock jar of honey for her greedy uncle. There was buttermilk and two of last night's cold boiled potatoes, still in their skins, for Bridgey's breakfast. She watched Sully walk up from the lake, shaking mud from his boots and muttering darkly to himself about the injustices of life. The mist had begun to disperse under a yellow late spring sun, and Bridgey could make out the Grimblett. It was lying just beneath the clear surface of the lake, all green and misty, spreading wavery tentacles far and wide across its realm.

'You look fit and well today, Grimblett, though I can tell you're angry with me Uncle Sully, and sure, why wouldn't you be? The way he sucks that dirty pipe and spits on you every day. I'll have to go now; he's coming for his breakfast. I'll talk to you later.'

Sully McConville sat across the table from his niece, watching her as he sucked tea noisily from a chipped mug. Bridgey kept her eyes down, munching industriously on the potatoes and washing them down with sips of buttermilk. Sully wiped his mouth on the back of his sleeve.

'Eat up now, girl, and thank the Lord who left me to provide for you after your ma and da passed on. Leave a clean plate now, and thank God for his goodness and bounty.'

He cracked an egg and spooned it hastily into his mouth, yellow runny yolk dribbling through the coarse whiskers on to his chin. Tearing a crust from the bread he dipped it in the honey and sucked noisily on it. Bridgey could not help the disgust which showed on her face. Sully wagged the crust at her across the table.

'Straighten your gob, girl, or I'll skelp the skin off your bones. Duck eggs are too rich for children and the honey would only bring you out in a rash of pimples. I need it for me chest.' Here he coughed to illustrate the point. 'Taters and buttermilk are what I was brought up on. They never harmed me, so you eat up now.'

'I will, Uncle.'

'And don't waste any. There's goodness in potato skins.'

'I'm not wasting any at all, Uncle.'

'Well make sure you don't.'

Bridgey would rather have died than eat a duck egg. The ducks were her friends and she had seen the ducklings that came from the eggs, little, downy, smiling creatures, with tiny comical wings. But white bread and honey, that was a different matter altogether. She had dipped soft white bread into the honey when her uncle was absent – it tasted like heaven on earth. Then one day Sully had caught her; he had beaten her soundly with a blackthorn stick he kept behind the door. Bridgey had never stolen bread and honey again, though she often dreamed of the bread, with its fresh smell and crispy crust, together with the sweet, heavy, mysterious stickiness of deep amber honey, with chewy fragments of combwax which clung to the teeth. Sully's voice broke in on her imaginings.

'Right, I'm off now to the Ballymain market. Mind you boil those taters the way I like them, so they're floury when they split. See to the ducks, put fresh straw in their pens, and tidy up around here. Sweep the floor, wash the dishes and scrub the table well. I'll be back at nightfall, and you know what'll happen to you if there's anything amiss, Bridgey.'

'You'll skelp the skin off me bones, Uncle.'

'Aye, so I will.'

Sully licked honey from his whiskers, belched, lighted his pipe and set his hat on squarely. Then he left for Ballymain market.

The afternoon was peaceful; under the warm sun the lake lay smooth and placid. Even the ducks had stopped paddling; they floated about silently, napping in the noontide. Mister Rafferty stood on the bank, gently squelching the mud under his webbed feet. Though he was facing away from the house his bright little eye oscillated backwards, as he watched Bridgey come to the water's edge, her bare feet disturbing the thin crust that the sun had baked upon the mud. Rafferty gave a short quack of welcome, declining to comment further on the loaf and honey crock which the little girl placed upon a stone. She sat down next to them. The drake wandered over, his slim graceful neck nodding slightly as he waddled. Bridgey passed her hand gently over his sleek head.

'Good afternoon to you, sir. Have you had enough of the swimming?'

Mister Rafferty nodded and settled down by her.

'Ah well, your family look all nice and peaceful there. See Matilda with her head beneath her wing, fast asleep, Lord love her.'

Drake and girl sat watching the water. Bridgey half closed her eyes and began intoning in a soft singsong voice.

'Grimblett, Grimblett, are you there?'

The lake stayed calm and unruffled.

'I know for sure you're out there, Grimblett. Will y'not bid me a good afternoon?'

Out upon the middle of the waters a single large bubble plopped and gurgled, causing ripples to widen across the surface. Bridgey and Mister Rafferty nodded knowingly.

'Ah, you're still angered over Sully spittin' and throwing sticks at you this morning.'

Once more the lake bubbled and gurgled. This time a frond of the heavy green weed that lay beneath the surface rose momentarily clear of the waters; then it slid back under. Bridgey sighed. 'Well I'm sorry for you, but there's little Rafferty or I can do.'

A huge bubble, like an upturned bathtub, gurgled its way into the noon air; more ripples began, stretching in circles until small waves lapped over Bridgey's toes. She stood up.

'I'll tell you what I'll do, Grimblett. I'll pour a bit of this honey to you, some bread and all. That should make you feel better, eh?'

This time the lake lay still.

Bridgey broke the bread and scattered it on the water. Immediately the ducks came awake and swam over to gobble it up, though Mister Rafferty remained faithfully at her side. Bridgey picked up the honey crock.

'Oh come on now, Grimblett, don't be sulking on such a fine afternoon. See, you were too late to get the bread, now Mister Rafferty's family've eaten it. Here, try some honey. You'll like it, the taste is like flowers and meadows in summer. Come on now.'

Bridgey tilted the crock, shaking it vigorously to make the honey flow. Rafferty watched her intently. The honey did not seem too keen on leaving its container, though a very small amount oozed out on to Bridgey's fingers. She licked the stickiness and rinsed her hands in the lake, cajoling her friend the Grimblett.

'Ah c'mon now, don't be shy. You'll enjoy it.'

Upending the crock, she shook it hard. The smooth glazed earthenware jar shot from between her wet hands and rolled away underwater down the steep lake bed before Bridgey could do anything about it. She slumped on the stone, holding her hands across her eyes, trying not to believe what she had just done.

'Heaven preserve me, Uncle Sully will skelp the skin off me bones with his blackthorn stick. I know he will, he'll have me very life! Grimblett, is there nothing you can do to save a little maid? Roll the crock back to me. Oh please!'

The water bubbled apologetically and lay calm. Mister Rafferty placed his bill sympathetically in Bridgey's lap as his family paddled close in and floated there, watching her. Slow minutes of the sunny noontide ebbed inexorably away. Bridgey's tears flowed along with them.

* * *

Nothing could hold back time and the return of Sully McConville from Ballymain market. Bridgey had cried herself to sleep by the lake; she wakened with the slight chill of advancing eventide to a reddening sky in which the sun sank gloriously, like a peach dipped into port wine. Hurrying to the house Bridgey rushed about like a dervish, setting the pot of potatoes on its tripod over the fire and tossing in a dash of salt. As if to redeem her quivering flesh from the crime she had committed the little girl set about her chores with furious energy, piling turf on the fire, scrubbing the table, sweeping the hard packed earth floor with a besom until dust flew widespread, wiping that same dust from shelf, table, chair and windows with a cheese-cloth. She put just the right amount of leaves into the battered teapot and trimmed the lamp wick to even the flame as darkness fell. Inside, the cottage was as fresh as new paint. Bridgey stood at the open door, her heart beating fitfully against the leaden weight within her chest as she watched her Uncle Sully staggering up the path through the darkness.

It was evident that he had been drinking by the way he weaved to and fro. Under his arm Sully carried a bottle and a piece of smoke-cured bacon from Ballymain market, to supplement his supper of boiled potatoes. He brushed past Bridgey and sat heavily in his chair, slamming down the bacon upon the table.

'Bridgey, slice some of this up an' fry it for me, a man needs some meat now and again. It's no good for chil-dren, mind, too fat an' salty. Well, don't stand there gawpin' with cow's eyes, move yourself, girl, or it'll be mornin' soon.'

With trembling hands she cut the bacon into rough slices, setting it on the frying pan to sizzle as she drained off the water from the potatoes . . . fearful that any moment her uncle might call for bread and honey. Sully, however, was not looking to satisfy his sweet tooth, not while there was whiskey to be had. Weary and footsore after the long trek home from Ballymain, he kicked off his boots and pulled the chair up to the fire. Lighting his clay pipe with a spill he started drink-ing straight from the bottle. Bridgey worked with quick, nervous energy, laying out his plate of food at the table and pouring a mug of tea for him. She gave a fearful start at the sound of Sully's voice.

'Is that the ducks I can hear still out on the lake, girl?'

'Ducks? Oh I must have forgotten, I'll get them into the pen right away. Come and have your supper, Uncle Sully. It's on the table, all nice and hot.'

He swigged at the bottle. His pipe lay forgotten on the hearth.

'I'll Uncle Sully you, idle little faggot. Never mind the supper, you get those ducks in or I'll skelp the skin off your bones!'

* * *

Bridgey fled the cottage, hurrying through the night to the water's edge. Mister Rafferty stood on the bank. Cocking his head on one side he quacked wearily. Bridgey could make out the shapes of other ducks, asleep on the far bank.

'Oh Mister Rafferty, there you are. I'm sorry I forgot to take you and your family to the pens. You've not been fed either. 'Tis all me own fault, I'm a terrible girl.'

The drake stretched himself, spreading his wings he quacked aloud his various complaints. Bridgey cast an uneasy glance at the cottage. 'Hush now, or you'll have me uncle out here with his great stick. Listen, we'll never get those others off the far bank until morning. You bide here and hold your noise, I've got to go back to the house. I promise you'll come to no harm, the Grimblett will watch over you and your family, I know he will.'

Mister Rafferty settled his neck down on his crop feathers as Bridgey ran off into the darkness. Behind him the surface of the lake threw up a few bubbles

65

before subsiding into the calm of a late spring night.

Bridgey breathed a small sob of relief; Uncle Sully had fallen asleep in his chair by the fire. Carefully she removed the quarter full whiskey bottle from between his limp fingers and set it on the table, alongside the now cold bacon and potatoes. It was not unusual for him to sleep all night in front of the fire, fully dressed, after he had been drinking. Safe for the night at least, Bridgey backed up the fire with damp slow-burning turf. Taking some potatoes in a clean piece of cloth she went back to the lake with an old shawl wrapped about her shoulders. Sully McConville snored gently, his mouth half open, chin on chest and hands lying loosely upon his stomach as it heaved up and down in the flickering shadows of the warm room.

Out by the lake Bridgey perched on a stone, sharing her meal of cold cooked potato with Mister Rafferty. A thin moon sliver hung over the lake like a slice of lemon rind, turning the water to a light golden shimmer, backed by the silhouette of the trees which massed on the far lakeshore. Bridgey murmured softly to her friend, 'There's a fear in me for what the morn will bring. I wish it could stay peaceful night forever, so I do.'

Beside her the drake blinked his bright little eyes and smiled that secret smile that only ducks and drakes know the meaning of.

* * *

Sully groaned aloud as morning sunlight cascaded through the window panes to set his brain afire. Flaming orange motes danced a jig before his half opened eyes; sour whiskey taste clogged his furred tongue as his temples thrummed with the father of all headaches. In a petulant croak he called out, 'Bridgey, bring the honey, girl!'

There was no answer, Sully heaved himself painfully out of his chair. The embers of the fire were hidden beneath thick grey ash. With ill-tempered bile rising within him he glared at the cold teapot beside the cold bacon and potatoes on the table. Tripping over his boots he cursed and kicked at them.

'Bridgey, bring me the honey an' a spoon, or I'll skelp the skin off your bones. Bridgey, where are y'girl?'

Stumbling and muttering he searched shelf and cupboard for the crock, longing for the soothing sweetness of honey to drive away the whiskey bitterness from his mouth. The quacking of unfed ducks down at the lake diverted his attention. He fumbled with the latch and swung the door ajar, wincing at the stream of sunlight which shafted in like a volley of golden arrows.

There she was, the idle little faggot, curled up on a stone with a shawl around her and that cheeky ould drake. This time he would teach her a lesson that she'd remember to her dying day!

Snatching the blackthorn stick from behind the door he roared like a wounded lion.

'Bridgeeeeeeee!'

Like a shot the little girl sprang up. Mister Rafferty, quacking and ruffled, slid from her knees awkwardly. Bridgey's face went white with fright at the sight of her uncle brandishing the blackthorn stick as he strode barefoot toward her.

'Er, er, top of the mornin' to you, sir, I was about to

feed the ducks.'

A large vein stood out on Sully's temple, pulsing like a nightingale's throat. His voice was thick and harsh.

'Feed the ducks, is it? What about me, don't I get fed? The place is like a midden – cold food, no fire, no tea or honey, and you out here sleepin' your shiftless life away!'

Sully had begun moving this way and that, cutting off any possible retreat. Bridgey had the lake at her back. There was no way she might avoid a skelping.

'Uncle, I'm sorry, it wasn't my fault. Me hands were wet an' the honey crock slipped off into the water. I'll never do it again.'

Sully smiled wickedly, raising the heavy stick.

'So, you'll not do it again, eh girl. You'll be lucky if you have legs to stand on after I'm done with you, me lazy scut!'

He swung the stick in a vicious arc. Bridgey dodged to one side. Sully slipped and fell heavily in the mud; he came up shouting and covered in brown slime.

'Cummere, I'll skelp the skin off your bo—'

And then Mister Rafferty was upon him, quacking and flapping. As if on a given signal the ducks came out with a rush from the water and piled in on Sully. Bridgey could hardly make out her uncle – he was enveloped in hissing, quacking, feather-beating, web-clawing birds. Sully lost the blackthorn stick in the mud, frantically he beat about, his arms milling wide, slipping, falling, skidding in the slutchy mud as he ranted and roared.

'I'll kill yeh, d'you hear me! I'll wring your blasted necks!'

Out in the middle of the lake bubbles began bursting on the surface. Bridgey cried aloud in terror.

'Save us, Grimblett! Oh do something, please!'

Sully thrust the birds from him with a mighty effort and stepped backward to gain a breathing space.

But he stepped back into the lake!

He slid in the sloping shallows and overbalanced. Blowing water from his nostrils and wiping his face upon a wet sleeve he stood there, his clawing hands shaking at Bridgey.

'I'll throttle the life from yeh, you and those ducks!'

The lake behind Sully McConville began bubbling madly, as if the waters were boiling. He tried pulling himself forward but slid further backwards. Something was wrapped around his feet; he felt the water lapping about his chest. A look of fear crossed his ugly features.

'Bridgey, help me, girl. Help me!'

Now the thick, trailing green fronds appeared. They draped about his arms and neck, caressing him with coldness they had fetched up from the depths. Sully tried feebly to fight against them, but they piled upon him like the tentacles of some unknown emerald monster. Colossal bubbles created waves upon the lake that filled his mouth and flooded his ears.

'Save me, girl, Bridgeeeeeee!'

She watched, fascinated, as a waving sloppy frond wrapped itself around her uncle's mouth and nostrils, stifling his cries forever. Back, back he was dragged until he vanished beneath the surface. The waters gave one final bulking swirl; a single bubble burst up from the depths into the sunlight. Then calm reigned over the scene. To any passing traveller it would have made a charming rustic picture: the little ragged girl standing in the sunshine with her ducks on the banks of a quiet lake.

* * *

Sully McConville's boots burned merrily on the turf fire. Bridgey sat in his chair, Mister Rafferty at her feet like a faithful pet dog. Ducks perched on the shelf, windowsill and table, some of them eating the remains of the cold potatoes from the supper plate. Bridgey stirred the drake gently with her bare foot.

'Mister Rafferty, d'you think you could tell your family to lay lots of eggs? Then in a day or two perhaps you and me will go to Ballymain market and get more honey, white bread too. You'd like that, wouldn't you? Sure it's grand stuff the honey is.'

She rose and went to lean on the windowsill, gazing out at the lake. 'And yourself, Grimblett, we'll bring honey back for you and all. Sure, it'll help you to get rid of the nasty taste, so it will.'

MY BROTHER GETS LETTERS

Michael Rosen
★ illustrated by Quentin Blake ★

My brother gets letters – not many, but some,
I don't know why – but I get none.
Odd people seem to write to him –
a card to say his bike's done or a library book's in.
He seems to have friends, who when they're away
write about their holiday,
like – 'We're near the beach, – had chips last night,
my bed squeaks and sand fleas bite.'
And sometimes he gets letters out of the blue
from people who can't know who they're writing to
offering him *The Reader's Digest Bird Book* cheap
or adverts for films like 'The Blobs' – GIANT JELLIES THAT
EAT AS THEY CREEP.

But I don't get anything. No-one writes to me.
That is – until just recently.

You see I was looking at the paper one day
and I was reading about this man's brain – it was
    fading away.
That is – until he had done this 'Memory Course'
and discovered his Inner Mind Force.
And when you got down to the end
It said: 'This sounds GREAT – please send
to me at this address now:
"SO YOU WANT TO SAVE BRAIN-CELLS? – HERE'S HOW".'
And you filled in your name and address along dotted
    lines
and sent it off to: 'Great Minds
P.O. Box 16, Manchester 8.'
It was as simple as that. Sit and wait.

Now as it happens I wasn't very worried about my
    Inner Mind Force
or the ones to cure baldness or put me on a slimming
    course,
but the thing was – they all had something for free
which they promised they'd send – addressed to me.
What could be better?
I'd get a letter.
So after I'd got some of these forms together
I came back then to my brother
and I said: 'I bet, out of us two,
I get more letters than you.'
And he said: 'Rubbish, no-one ever writes to you,
you're a Nobody, a No-one-knows-who.'

'Right,' I said, 'we'll keep a score,
me and you – see who gets more.'
'Great,' he said, and shook my hand. 'Done!
What do I get,' he said, 'when I've won?'
'No prizes,' I said. 'But whoever loses,
will have to do whatever the winner chooses.'
'Great,' he said again – and laughed,
he must have thought I was daft
to take him on.
He thought he couldn't go wrong.
'I'll show him,' I thought. 'What I can't wait to see
is his face when these people write back to me.'

So anyway, I sent off about three or four
and soon I got what I was hoping for.
A former Mr Universe had written to say:
'BUILD POWER-PACKED MUSCLES
in just 70 seconds a day!!!'
'There you are,' I said to my brother.
'A letter – One nil – and tomorrow I'll be getting another.'
So while he read what they had sent me
'Rippling muscles on guarantee
see your strength rise
right before your very eyes
on the built-in POWER-METER,'
I sat tight for my next letter.
Next to come through the post was Harvey Speke.
'I see my years of fatness as a past nightmare I'll never
    repeat.
Why be fat when you can be slim?
Shrink your waistline, stomach and chin,
I used to look like THIS – believe it or not!'

73

And there were pictures of bellies and heaven knows
    what
before and after shrinking with the Miracle Pill.
I didn't read the rest – 'Two nil!'
I said to my brother. 'I'm winning, aren't I?
You can't win now.' But he says: 'Oh can't I?'
and I can see he's getting really angry
reading about pills to stop you feeling hungry.

Next day there were two more –
one was a rather glossy brochure
on an Old Age Pension Plan
and the other on Shoes For The Larger Man.
For three days he hadn't got anything through the
    post.
He sat there at breakfast munching his toast
staring at his plate while I was making a neat stack

of leaflets and letters I'd got back.
'Four nil now, isn't it? Give in?
You see,' I said, 'every day I'm getting something.'
And sure enough *something* arrived not long after
but it wasn't quite what I was after.

It was a great big parcel – it had come from Liverpool.
'Who's it for?' I said. 'You, you fool.'
It was the first parcel I'd ever had in my life.
'Go on – open it,' father said, 'here's a knife.'
And they all stood round to see who'd sent a parcel to
   me.
Even my brother wanted to see.
It was wrapped in red paper but the box was brown.
I pulled the lid off – and it was an eiderdown.
It was what is nowadays called a Quilt for a bed,
But we used to call them 'eiderdowns', instead.

'What is it?' 'A pillow?'

'Who sent it?' 'I don't know.'

'How much did it cost you?' 'What do you mean?'

'Don't be funny – he hasn't got a bean.'

I panicked. I came over cold.

Don't forget – I was only nine years old.

'Did you send off for this thing?'

'No,' I said. 'All I did was fill a form thing in,

it said there was something for free –

fill in the form and it'd come to me.'

'Fat-head! That means free till the seventh day,

keep it longer than that and you've got to pay.

Send it back if you don't.

Mind you – I bet you won't.'

'Don't say that,' said mother, 'he wasn't to know
 better.'

'But what was he doing?' 'I wanted a letter.'

'Well get your friend Mart to send you cards from
 Wales when he goes

instead of sending off for boxes of bed-clothes.'

I felt such an idiot looking at the eiderdown.

I looked at my brother. He looked round.

'What's the matter? Five nil. Well done.'

He laughed. 'I think you've won

or do you want to go on for a bit more?'

'No no no,' I said, 'I don't care about the score.'

'So you'll wrap up the box and send it back?' father
 said.

'Unless you want to pay for a new eiderdown on your
 bed.'

But I didn't do it straightaway,

and I didn't do it the next day,

or the next, or the next,
the eiderdown and the wrapping were in a gigantic
  mess.
'The eiderdown's growing,' I was thinking,
'No! The box to send it back in's shrinking.'
Anyway fourth day on – eiderdown still not sent
we were all having tea – the doorbell went.

My brother looks up. 'Probably the police –
on the hunt for an eiderdown thief.'
Father went to see who was there
and we could hear voices from where we were.
Moment later – he's back – very long in the face,
he looks at me. 'It's for you,' he says.
I could have died. 'Is it the police
on the hunt for an eiderdown thief?'
'No,' he says, 'there's a man out there.
He's got something for you.' 'Out where?
Men don't come round here for me.'
But I went to the door and they all followed to see.
'Mr Rosen, is it?' The man looked.
He was reading my name out of a black book.
'No,' I said. 'You want my father.'
'*M*. Rosen?' he says. 'He's *H*, I gather.'
I said, 'Yes. I'm M.'
So he says, 'Good. Right then,
it's outside. Shall I wheel it in?'
'What?' I said. 'The washing machine.'
'Washing machine? Oh no. Not for me.'
'Well it says here "*M*. Rosen", all right. Do you want to
  see?'
'No,' I said, 'I only send for free things.'

'Yes, the demonstrations *are* free,' he says, 'but not the
   washing machines.'
'I don't want it.' I looked round for help.
You can imagine how I felt.
But they were hiding behind the door
laughing their heads off – my brother on the floor.
I turned back. Looked up at the man.
'I've brought it now,' he says. 'It's in the van.'
'I've come all the way from Hoover's to show it you.'
'No,' I said. 'No?' he said. 'Haven't you got anyone
   else I could show it to?'
For a moment – it felt like a week –
he looked down at me – I looked down at my feet.
Then he shut his book and went, and I shut the door,
and straightaway my brother was there with 'Shall I
   add that to your score?
Six nil? Have you won yet?'
I said, 'I've had enough of this letter bet.'
And he said, 'Why? Don't you want a washing
   machine?
You could use it to keep your eiderdown clean!'
'Oh no! The eiderdown.' For a moment I'd forgotten
   about it.
'I can't get it in. The box: – it's shrunk!' I shouted.
But mum said, 'I'll help you send that back, don't
   worry,
but what's coming next? A coat? A lorry?'
But father said, 'Who's won this bet?
And what's the winner going to get?'
My brother looked really happy and said, 'I've lost –
Letters? *He's* the one that gets the most.'
'All I want,' I said, 'is I don't want to hear any more

about it.
If I have to send off to get a letter – I'm better off with-
  out it.'
'OK,' my brother said, 'let's call it square.'
'Yes,' I said, 'we'll leave it there.'

But even now –
when there's someone asking for me at the door,
who mum has never seen before,
she says to me: 'It's for you, dear.
Quick! Your eiderdown's here!'

THE GULF

Geraldine McCaughrean

The cold, thin air in the back of his throat was like swallowing swords, but he ran until sweat burst through his skin, until the sweat dried to salt. He ran until every searchlight, floodlight and white-winking barrack window was out of sight and he was running in utter darkness. He ran until night gave way to morning, and every moment he expected to hear shouts or motors or the barking of dogs on his trail.

With sunrise he allowed his hopes to rise too, like a hot, orange ball of flame within his chest. Might he after all make good his escape? Might he reach safety, against all the odds? No-one ever did, they had told him. No-one ever would. But the hope kept rising in his throat until it buckled his mouth into a smile.

Then he reached the gulf.

He almost ran straight into it – a gorge of such dizzying depth that the river in the bottom was only a green thread; a canyon so wide that a horse at full gallop could not have leapt even halfway across. And its sides were sheer.

Juan fell to his knees, grazing his forehead on the bark of a dead, fallen tree, his arms over his head. Had he come this far to meet disappointment like a snake across his path? There was no way over. The gulf stretched as far as the eye could see to right and left. He could leap into it or wait at the brink of his pursuers to catch up with him. But he was done for. It was true. No-one ever escaped. No-one ever would.

When he raised his head, Juan saw a little girl watching him. She stood on the far side of the canyon, rubbing a twist of grass between her hands. 'Want to cross over?' she said. In the silence of the empty landscape her voice floated easily over to him. She did not have to shout.

She spoke the dialect of the neighbouring country. The river gorge must be the border, then. Juan had reached the border – a stone's throw from safety. 'Is there a bridge? Anywhere? A bridge?' he called.

'No. No bridge . . . But I could fetch my sisters.' She put her fingers in her mouth and whistled shrilly. Juan gave a laugh somewhere between a bark and a sob. Much good her sisters would do him.

The girls came dawdling out from the long grass and regarded him with the same solemn brown eyes. Each was rubbing a twist of grass between her hands.

'He wants to cross over,' said the sister.

'Better tell the brothers,' they said.

Ten boys emerged from the swashing grass, carrying sickles and armfuls of grass. They sat down on the far side of the ravine, dangling their legs over the rim. Their hands began to work in that same nervous, habitual motion, rubbing the grass stems together into long tasselled cords.

'Go home,' said Juan, glancing over his shoulder. He did not want them to witness either his tears or his recapture. He had no idea how much of a lead he had gained on his pursuers. Eight hours? Nine?

'They chasing you?' called one of the boys, swatting flies.

'I thought I could reach the border. But the gulf . . . I didn't know . . .'

Their sunburned faces expressed no sympathy, no sadness at his predicament. Their small brown hands just went on twisting grass.

'I'll tell the mothers,' said the littlest boy, and ran off, his bare feet unsettling flies in clouds.

The village must have been just over the ridge, for he soon returned, towing his mother by the hand. For the first time, Juan realized that the grass-twirling was not a nervous habit but a livelihood. The mothers – handsome women with shining plaits to which their babies clung – were also twirling the grass together into fibres, their big hands worn horny by the coarse stems. They contemplated Juan with large, dark-fringed eyes. 'You need help,' said one.

Juan laughed hollowly. 'I am past helping. This gulf did for me.'

The women called the children together, took their cords of grass, and began, simply by rubbing, to splice the thin lengths into thicker, longer ones. 'Fetch the grandmas and grandpas,' they told the littlest boy.

Away he went, and fetched back with him the old people of the village – mumbling, bent, bone-weary old bodies who shook their heads and clutched their shawls round them, even though the day was hot. One old matriarch, her hat as big as a bundle of laundry, flumped down amid her skirts, and the women laid their grass-cords at her feet, as if paying homage. Her whispering palms twirled their individual cords into one long rope, with a deftness which defied belief. For a few blessed minutes Juan watched with such intent fascination that he forgot his own peril and strained to make out what magical process, what cunning craftmanship could twist grass into rope.

Then, with a jolt of hope sharp as a kick, he realized that the rope was for him – to get him over the ravine.

What well-meaning, simple fools! Inwardly he raged with bitter laughter. Even if they succeeded in making a cable strong enough to carry the weight of a man, long enough to span the gulf, how would they get the end across to him? Impossible! So much work and for what? Around him the evening breeze sprang up, and Juan found he had sat all day by the gulf watching the children and grandparents and mothers opposite labour over the rope, which now lay coiled at the old woman's feet.

That same breeze carried on it the sound of jeep engines, of sirens, of his pursuers.

'What's the point? What's the point?' he bawled, and his voice dropped into the ravine like a rock fall.

The little girl – the one he had seen first – lifted up a coil of the immense rope to show him. It was all she could do to raise it off the ground. 'Father will help,' she said. 'He is coming soon.'

It reduced him to tears – this little mite's touching, ridiculous trust in her father. What would he prove to be, after all, but yet another pigeon-chested peasant in a straw hat, chewing betel nuts and hoping for a quiet life. A man like Juan.

The little girl's father proved, however, to be a big,

energetic man – a hunter. When he arrived, his jeans and shirt dusty after a day on the plateau, he found the village assembled by the ravine, saw Juan, saw the rope, and instantly re-strung his bow. His grandmother threaded a needle with sewing thread, and stuck it through the grass rope, then gave the thread to her grandson. He tied it to his arrow and, without a word to Juan . . . fired it straight at him.

The arrow gouged up the soil between Juan's feet. With trembling fingers, he snatched the cotton, winding the loops so tight round his hand that his fingers went blue. The rope was heavy, but the sewing thread did not break. Like a great anaconda, the rope's end sagged its way across the ravine, and Juan made it fast around the log. The strongest of the villagers took hold of the other end and braced themselves.

The jeeps were visible now, bouncing over the rough terrain, the evening sun flashing on their windscreens. In the normal way of things, Juan could never have brought himself to do what he did next. But after so many people had done so much, he could hardly hesitate. Hanging like a tree sloth under the grass rope he crabbed his way over the yawning, heart-numbing terror of the vertiginous drop, fixing all his thoughts on the beauty of the hawser, the thousand different shades of yellow and green all interwoven into one speckled cable. How could something so strong be made of such frail component parts? The seed-dust made him sneeze.

The jeeps skidded to a halt just as hands – old and young and callused – closed in Juan's hair and round his arms and through his belt and pulled him to safety.

Then the villagers dropped their end of the great rope into the ravine. It thumped against the far wall, shedding a shower of seeds.

Juan jumped to his feet and shook a defiant fist at the men on the opposite bank. In his raised hand was a single twist of grass.

THE BOY WHO WALKED ON WATER

Vivian French

★ illustrated by Chris Fisher ★

Once there was a boy who could walk on water. He lived with his grandfather and his mother on an island where the sea crept into the land with long twisting fingers, and rivers and streams wound round and round and in and out until the island was a patchwork of rocks and hills and fields sewn together with strips of shining water.

Although the island was small it was not easy to travel from East to West, or North to South, for there were always saltwater lakes to walk around or rivers or streams to cross. The boy, Fergal, had no such problem. As soon as he could walk at all he walked as easily on water as he did on the ground. He walked on the streams and the lakes and the rivers, and even the sea. 'Look at that,' said his mother. 'Now, there's a gift.' His grandfather said nothing. He was a fisherman, as were all the islanders, and he had seen and thought many things while he was rocking in his boat on the northern seas. A grandson who could walk on water was certainly strange, but there was, most likely, a reason for it somewhere.

When Fergal was a little boy he did not notice that he was different from other children. After all, every winter, when cold winds came sweeping down from the North, the sea froze, and the lakes and rivers and streams of the island turned into solid blocks of clouded silver ice. All the children whooped and slithered and slid, and Fergal slid with them. Even when the spring came and the ice and snow melted away, Fergal played happily with his friends. Some of them were good at running races. Others were expert at walking on wooden stilts. Ailsa could swing herself round and round in cartwheels. Fergal could walk on water. If the older children looked at him strangely and whispered behind their hands, Fergal never noticed. The adults said nothing at all. They agreed with Fergal's grandfather. There was probably a reason somewhere, and if there wasn't, well, it did the boy no harm, nor anyone else as far as they could see.

* * *

As Fergal grew, things changed, and not for the better. He was a shy, quiet boy who wanted nothing more than to be like everyone else – but no-one else could do what he did. Two or three children began to tease him, and soon, the others joined in.

'Fergal's a water beetle!' they called after him.

Their parents told them to leave Fergal alone. 'He can't help the way he is,' they said. 'Don't bother him.' But the children took no notice. They ran after Fergal and danced in circles round him.

'Fergal the frog!' 'Maybe he's been bewitched!' 'He's not like us!' 'Fergal's STRANGE!'

Ailsa slipped her hand into his, and told him not to mind.

* * *

Fergal became quieter still, and more thoughtful. His mother noticed that he now hopped across the stream on the stepping-stones, and walked all the way down to the bridge to cross the river. When it was warm enough to splash and swim in the sea Fergal was nowhere to be seen.

'Where have you been?' Ailsa asked him.

'I had to help my mother in the house,' Fergal told her, but his mother was sitting down on the harbour's edge mending nets.

As time went by the children slowly forgot that Fergal had once been able to walk on water. All they remembered was that he was in some way different, and however hard he tried he was never at the centre of the laughing groups of boys and girls. Only Ailsa called for him to join them as they ran races on the sand or jumped from rock to rock. Only Ailsa caught his hand and dragged him into games of tag or catch-me-as-you-can. If Ailsa was busy looking after her little brothers and sisters Fergal was left alone. He would go for long solitary walks North and South and East and West, but he never once walked on water.

'Be careful,' his grandfather told him. 'Gifts are given to be used, not to be hidden.'

Fergal turned away.

* * *

The storm came early one morning as the last fishing boat sailed into the harbour. It was the most terrible storm that the islanders had ever lived through; far

89

more wild than the storm that had drowned Fergal's father on the day that Fergal was born. Black clouds came swirling up and covered the island in darkness, and tearing winds wrenched bushes out of the earth and hurled them into the air. For three days and nights the sea roared and growled and clawed at the island until the shores and cliffs were raw and ragged. The fishermen's boats were snatched from the harbour and tossed into the howling tempest as if they were walnut shells, and the huge rocks and slabs of granite that made up the harbour wall were cracked and splintered until they lurched broken into the heaving waves around them.

* * *

When at last the storm was over the islanders walked silently down to the shore. They did not speak. There was nothing to say. There was no harbour, no protecting wall and not one boat. The younger children ran about picking up strips of seaweed and scraps of sailcloth that lay scattered on the sand and stones, but the older ones looked anxiously at their parents.

'Will we build the harbour again?' a boy asked his father.

His father shook his head. 'What for?' he said, and his voice was bleak. 'We have no boats to keep there.'

'We can find wood and make more boats,' said a girl.

Her mother sighed. 'You know there are no trees here. We trade our fish for wood . . . and without our boats there will be no fish.'

'No fish, and nothing else besides,' said an old man. 'All our livelihood is gone. There's nothing left for us now.'

'Look! Look!'

Ailsa's father had climbed out on the cliff above the tumbled heaps of stone where the harbour wall had stood. Now he was shouting and waving his arms. 'A boat!' he shouted. 'I can see a boat!' Other islanders rushed to join him, and Ailsa and Fergal scrambled after them. They shaded their eyes and stared over the sea, and wondered about the dark speck way out across the heaving and rolling waves.

'Whatever it is we must fetch it in!' said Ailsa's father. 'If it's nothing but wreckage we can save the wood . . . and if it is a boat we can begin again! We can search for our fishing boats . . . we can fish . . . we can live!' And he tore off his heavy boots and coat and leapt down the cliff to plunge into the cold water.

'No! No!' Ailsa ran after her father, but she was too late. He was already striding deeper and deeper into the swell of the tide. An incoming wave knocked him off balance and Ailsa gasped as he sank beneath the steel grey water, but he came up spluttering. He was still looking ahead to the horizon. The islanders watched silently as he began to swim with short jerky strokes. None of them were strong or able swimmers. They believed, like most fishermen, that it was better to drown quickly than to swim on and on and die a slow and lingering death.

* * *

Ailsa's face was white. Even as her father stared steadily ahead of him so she watched her father. His black head, glistening like a seal, moved further and further away from the shore and safety.

Fergal looked at Ailsa, and then out across the

91

rippling sea. Was it a boat? If it was, it was tossing and teasing at the edge of sight. Surely no-one could swim so far. Fergal turned, and walked to the water's edge. As he stepped out from the sand there was a roar from the rocks above. 'Murdo's in trouble! He's sinking! He can't go any further!'

No-one saw Fergal take his first step. They were far too intent on shouting and calling to Ailsa's father to see that Fergal, for the first time in his life, was paddling – that he was not walking on water but splashing in the shallow lapping waves. Fergal stood still. His gift was gone.

'Fergal! FERGAL!' It was Ailsa, flying down the shore towards him. 'Fergal – save him! Save my father!'

'Go, boy, go!' His grandfather was beside him. 'Now's the time, Murdo's drowning! Help him, boy, help him! Walk on water!'

Fergal took another step, and the waves splashed against him so that he stumbled. He turned, his face white as Ailsa's, and held out his hands. 'Ailsa!' he said. 'It won't work for me any more!'

Ailsa stared at him, her eyes wide.

'You do it,' said Fergal, and he touched her arm. 'Walk on water, Ailsa – GO!'

And Ailsa was walking on the water. She was walking, she was running, she was skimming the surface like a seagull.

The islanders held their breath as she flew over the tossing waves, over the white foam. She reached her father as he struggled to the surface for the third time, coughing and gasping, his lungs bursting with the desire for air. Ailsa reached down to him, and there were the two of them standing hand in hand on the water as if it were nothing more than a shifting sheet of glass under their feet. Together they turned to the horizon.

* * *

All the men and women and children standing on the cliff top stared. They rubbed their eyes and wondered if they had really seen what they thought they had seen. They shook their heads and told each other that the mist was coming up over the sea, and it was easy to see strange things in mist. They told the children not to be so foolish. How could they imagine that two people could walk together on water, hand in hand? But all the same, Ailsa and her father were gone. Had they both drowned? Or would they come back? Could they come back?

* * *

'We'll watch and wait,' said Fergal's grandfather, and it was agreed that this was all that could be done.

* * *

It was almost dark when Ailsa and her father came back to the island. The sun was sinking low into the West, and stars were creeping up the violet sky. The little boat came dancing over the waves with the evening wind behind it, its sail bellying out triumphantly. The islanders raised a cheer that shook the seabirds off the rocks, and hurried to haul the boat high up on the shingle. Ailsa and her father were carried shoulder high, up and away to where a fire was blazing on the headland to light them home. There was singing and dancing and feasting, and when Ailsa's father told how he and Ailsa had seen more of their boats beached

94

on a bare island not too far to the North the cheering reached the moon itself.

'Murdo has saved us all!' a boy shouted.

'Aye! Aye! Three cheers for Murdo and Ailsa!'

'Murdo who swam to save us!'

'Murdo the seal swimmer!'

Ailsa's father Murdo nodded his head, but Ailsa jumped up.

'We didn't swim!' she said. 'It was Fergal. Fergal gave me his gift! We walked on water!'

The islanders nodded and smiled at Ailsa, but they went on singing and celebrating. Soon it was understood that Murdo the seal swimmer had swum halfway across the ocean to save the island. And Ailsa? Some said Ailsa had swum after him . . . and a few said she walked on water. Most islanders shook their heads. Hadn't they told the same story of Fergal . . . and was that true? No!

* * *

Ailsa slipped away from the flickering lights of the fire. 'Fergal!' she called into the darkness, 'Fergal!'

There was no answer. Ailsa went down to the shore. Fergal was sitting on a stone, his feet in the water, listening to the waves as they whispered and sighed in and out of the little stones under his toes.

'Fergal!' said Ailsa, and she ran to him. 'Fergal, I've lost your gift! When Father and I found the boat it left us. Will it come back to you?'

Fergal shook his head. 'I don't think so,' he said, and he looked down. 'I don't want it. I've never known what water felt like before today. It feels like cold silk. It's so beautiful!'

Ailsa shivered. 'Beautiful,' she said, 'but dangerous too.'

Fergal picked up a pebble and tossed it into the water. It fell with a splash, and Ailsa laughed and threw another pebble after it. Then she caught at Fergal's hand, and pulled him to his feet. 'Come on,' she said. 'I can hear the fiddler playing up on the cliff. Come and dance!'

'We can dance here,' said Fergal, and he and Ailsa held hands and twirled and whirled round and round on the sandy shore. Neither of them noticed the pebbles as they bobbed back up to the surface of the sea as easily as if they were corks, and floated slowly away upon the outgoing tide.